MRS. POLLIFAX UNVEILED

Mrs. Pollifax
Unveiled

DOROTHY GILMAN

DOUBLEDAY DIRECT LARGE PRINT EDITION

BALLANTINE BOOKS • NEW YORK

A Ballantine Book
Published by The Ballantine Publishing Group

ISBN 0-7394-0764-3

Manufactured in the United States of America

**This Large Print Book carries the
Seal of Approval of N.A.V.H.**

*To Leona Nevler, who has been my editor
for more years than we'd care to admit . . .*

MRS. POLLIFAX UNVEILED

Prologue

Mrs. Pollifax was feeling bored and rather left out of life. Cyrus had recently accepted an invitation to teach law three days a week at the university; he was hugely enjoying it.

"Damned good to feel so useful again," he'd admitted, and she was glad for him.

She, however, was not feeling particularly useful. She reminded herself that she was still growing prizewinning geraniums, was in excellent health, hoped soon to earn her black belt in karate, and remained a faithful member of the Save Our Environment club. But . . . *How spoiled I am,* she thought. For a woman of what was delicately referred to as "of a certain age" she ought to feel fortunate indeed, and yet . . . She realized that she was absentmindedly scratching her left arm from which, not long ago, a bullet had been removed in a Bedouin tent by a man named Bushaq, and she concluded that what she was experiencing was letdown.

The price one pays, she thought sadly, for venturing out into dangerous worlds for Carstairs and the CIA, only to return to errands at the grocery store and bank, cooking and cleaning, mulching her garden for the winter, and pampering her geraniums.

Across the breakfast table from her, almost hidden behind his newspaper, Cyrus glanced up and saw the gesture toward her arm. "Still hurting?" he asked. "Do wish you'd let Dr. Orton have a look at that." He hesitated, and then, "Damn good to have you safe at home again, Em," and as he said this the telephone rang. He put down his cup of coffee, reached across his briefcase and newspaper, and when he answered it she saw his face change. Handing the phone to her he said, "It's Bishop."

"Oh," she said, startled, and concealing her reaction she kept her voice casual. "Bishop, how good to hear from you, are you well?"

Bishop, however, was not interested in polite conversation. He said bluntly, "Have any important plans for this day?"

"No," she said, honestly enough.

"A car will pick you up in forty minutes at your house," he said. "Carstairs wants to talk with you. Oh, and you might bring your passport with you, just in case."

And he hung up.

"Emily," said her husband warningly.

"He just wants to talk with me," she told him.

"Hard to believe," growled Cyrus. "You haven't even been home long enough for that arm to heal."

"It's healed," she told him. "It just itches."

He gave her a rueful smile. "I know, I know—I promised never to interfere, but still I don't like the sound of that call." With a glance at the clock on the wall he added, "And now I've got to go or I'll miss my first class, but Em—nothing dangerous, promise?"

He knew, of course, that anything Carstairs might have in mind could be dangerous; after all, she and Cyrus had met in Zambia under very dangerous circumstances and they had survived by luck and ingenuity. Cyrus had gone with her to Thailand, too, where he'd been snatched away from her by bandits, but she did not think it wise to remind him of this, nor to mention that Bishop had asked her to bring her passport. Instead she said tactfully, with a bright smile, "Barbecued chicken for dinner tonight," and when he had gone she hurried upstairs to dress for her trip to CIA headquarters.

1

Mrs. Pollifax, entering Carstairs's office, smiled at the many times she'd opened this same door, and wondered again why she'd been so hastily summoned by car and private plane. As she closed the door behind her, Carstairs's assistant, Bishop, glanced up from his desk and leaped to his feet to give her a hug. "Thank heaven you're here, Carstairs has been testy all morning."

"Testy, Bishop?"

"Grouchy. Impatient. Cross. If you'll wait I'll check my thesaurus for a stronger word."

"I'll pass on that," she told him dryly, and he opened the door to Carstairs's inner office. "She's here," he announced.

Carstairs rose from his desk to shake hands with her, tall and lean, his shock of white hair a sharp contrast to the tanned face that always mystified Bishop, who knew how seldom the man ventured outdoors, how much he despised exercise, and how often he worked long into the night.

"Relieved and delighted to see you, Mrs. P.," he said, smiling at the sight of her. It still amused him that one of his canniest agents was an untrained amateur, a woman who once, very naively, had arrived downstairs in Mason's office with a bland introduction from her congressman, and after bewildering poor Mason with polite questions had announced that she had *really* come to apply for work as a spy. Since then there had been moments when Carstairs shuddered at the thought that if he'd not passed Mason's office at the right moment and seen her sitting there—so perfect for a courier job he had in mind—Mason would have dismissed her and Carstairs would have missed the constant astonishment of her achievements, the assignments she'd pulled off so ingenuously and ingeniously through sheer instinct.

What he tended to forget, of course—and was conveniently overlooking now—was his heightened blood pressure when he thought her lost, captured or dead. "Very swashbuckling hat," he told her. "Do sit down and join us."

"Us?"

He gestured toward the opposite end of the room where a man in blue jeans and a tweed jacket stood with his back to them, peering closely at the huge map on the wall and tracing routes with one finger. When he turned from the map she gasped, *"Farrell?"*

"Hi, Duchess," said John Sebastian Farrell with a mischievous grin.

"But . . . what are you doing here? I thought you were back in Mexico City with your art gallery!"

"Sold it," he said, strolling over to join them. "My own paintings are selling damn well these days so I'm leaving both the gallery and Mexico."

"To work with Carstairs again?"

He gave her a kiss on the cheek. "Doubtful, Duchess, but Carstairs keeps hoping. At the moment . . ." He shrugged. "Strictly freelancing . . . you know how I am."

She smiled. "Yes, I do—restless," she said. Reckless, too, of course: undercover agent in Mexico for years, with gunrunning on the side . . . working with freedom fighters in Africa . . . and still too handsome for his own good. She turned back to Carstairs, who suggested they both sit down.

Once seated, Carstairs leaned back comfortably in his chair and said, "I need one respectable and indignant aunt to inquire about a missing niece, and a bodyguard to keep her out of trouble, and whose relationship we've not yet determined—friend or cousin—to accompany her."

Farrell winked at Mrs. Pollifax and she smiled and waited.

After studying their faces for a moment Carstairs nodded. "When the two of you flew off to the Middle East recently," he said, "you were neither of you on assignment for me. It was strictly Farrell's gig, keeping a promise to an old friend in trouble, but what the two of you happened to bring back for us at the department was a small miracle." He hesitated and then added with a rueful smile, "Now I'm hoping you both can produce a miracle again, but on *official* assignment, and for us."

"Where?" asked Farrell.

"The Middle East again, Syria this time. Today is Wednesday and I know you're available, but you, Mrs. Pollifax, would you be free to leave on Sunday?"

"For Syria?" In her mind Mrs. Pollifax ran over her engagements and nodded. "I'd need only cancel Garden Club on Monday, and my karate lesson on Tuesday. Yes, I could leave Sunday."

"Still brown belt?" inquired Carstairs with a smile.

When she nodded politely, still sensing amusement when the subject arose, he said, "Good—you've brought your passport with you? We'll need it for your visa."

"Yes, but why Syria?" she asked.

"Because a young American woman has mysteriously disappeared there. Actually she appears to have been kidnapped," he said, "and rather spectacularly. For weeks both the State Department and our embassy in Damascus have made the usual inquiries and protests, but there's been a lamentable lack of action, interest, information, or results. Syria," he added, "does not admit to allowing terrorist groups into the country."

Startled, Mrs. Pollifax said, "Terrorists? You mean you think they're involved in her disappearance?"

Carstairs nodded. "There's every reason to believe this, as you will see in a moment for yourselves."

"See?" echoed Mrs. Pollifax.

"And moreover there's been no ransom asked, which makes it even more of a mystery. The State Department has turned the job over to us now, to learn if possible where she might be, or find out what happened to her."

Mrs. Pollifax nodded. "Your department being more nefarious, devious and underhanded, of course, than the State Department?"

With a faint smile he ignored this. "Syria is a very safe country—for tourists," he emphasized, "but safe only because military service is mandatory, so you'll find armed soldiers on guard nearly everywhere, and because Syria has half a dozen intelligence agencies, of which the most feared are the secret police, the *mukhabarat*—"

"A group already familiar to us," put in Farrell dryly.

"—who have not taken our inquiries seriously either, but who just may take a great deal of interest in an indignant relative arriving to make inquiries and demand action. We'll have someone from the embassy in Damascus meet your plane, which should give you some protection in case of problems."

"But also call attention to us," pointed out Farrell.

"Oh yes, but in any case you'll be noticed and you'll need to practice care and caution. This is Hafiz al-Assad's country and he's a clever, shrewd, intelligent, and ruthless man, as witness his notorious massacre in the city of Hamah in 1982, at that time a hotbed of opposition by the Muslim Brotherhood. Some twenty thousand or more men, women and children were cut down and killed . . . not a pretty story but that's the Middle East. Since then there's been little need for al-Assad to worry about opposition—he's proved his power, which is why you'll find the country stable now . . . stable but stagnant.

"On the other hand," he added, "the country's stability is entirely due to Assad, and if anything should happen to him—as the United States is well aware—all hell could break loose in the Middle East. The country's a patchwork of minorities: Turks, Armenians, Jews, Kurds, Bedouin, Palestinians, with Muslims in the majority. Before Assad worked his way to the top there were something like twenty coups. Without him . . ." He shrugged. "Without him Assad's secular government could be taken over by Islamic radicals—which would alarm us very much—or Syria could be invaded by any of its neighboring countries—which would alarm us even more. You'll find the people themselves very friendly, but never forget it's a police state and completely under Assad's control."

"Are we likely to be under surveillance?" asked Farrell.

"Quite likely."

Mrs. Pollifax sighed. "I hate being followed, it's so inhibiting."

Carstairs smiled. "I think you'll manage somehow to divide and divert at the proper moments." He picked up the intercom and said, "We're ready now for the film, Bishop."

"Film?" said Farrell.

Carstairs nodded. "You'll be able to watch the entire event on film, in fact you may even have already seen this on CNN or your local newscast six weeks ago."

"Six weeks ago! But that leaves a cold trail," protested Farrell.

"Not necessarily. The time lag could also find her abductors relaxed and less guarded."

Bishop entered, walked to the huge map

on the wall, pressed a button, and a white screen descended over it, after which he dimmed the lights in the office and sat down.

Carstairs said, "This is October. The hijacking—and you may remember it—took place in August: an American plane on its way to Egypt was taken over by two hijackers at gunpoint, who ordered the pilot to take them to Syria."

Startled, Mrs. Pollifax said, "There was that girl—yes!"

Carstairs nodded. "The plane did land in Damascus, as ordered—it had to because it ran out of fuel—and it then spent a day on the tarmac while negotiations proceeded, but the ending was not at all to the satisfaction of the hijackers." With a nod to Bishop he said, "You can start the film now. Her name, by the way, was Amanda Pym."

"Was?" said Mrs. Pollifax.

"Is, we hope."

The film began with a camera trained on two people being interviewed in an airport terminal, a small audience watching in the background, among them armed police in khaki, and above them, in the distance, a huge picture of President Hafiz al-Assad.

The two objects of attention were a plain-looking young woman who was being congratulated on saving the lives of 203 passengers, and an American soldier.

"Hold it a minute," said Carstairs, and Bishop froze the film for a closer look at the young woman.

"Oh dear," murmured Mrs. Pollifax.

"Oh dear *what?*" inquired Carstairs.

"She's so—so colorless," she said, and wondered what she had expected. "Where does she come from? Her clothes are all wrong—as if she found them at a yard sale—and much too big for her."

"She's who you'll be looking for," Carstairs reminded her.

"Yes," said Mrs. Pollifax, and began to memorize carefully the round young face that was framed by straight, mouse-colored hair. No lipstick. Wide gray eyes—was there a flash of resentment in them at being questioned? "Perhaps she's shy," concluded Mrs. Pollifax.

"Her eyes are attractive," Farrell said politely, "but it's true, that brown suit, circa 1950, is too big for her. Bad advice from *someone.*"

Carstairs said curtly, "If you've finished criticizing her appearance . . ."

"Sorry," said Farrell meekly.

". . . we'll start the film again."

Amanda Pym had been asked a question and her reply was so mumbled it was inaudible. The army sergeant next to her broke in to say eagerly, "A real heroine she is. All of us scared to death—I admit I was, too. I mean, they'd been threatening to kill us—shoot us one by one—if they weren't allowed a safe exit, but Miss Pym—well, she suddenly got up from her seat in the back—I heard people whispering, 'For God's sake, get *down,*'—but she just walked up to the hijacker nearest her—his back was turned—tapped him on the shoulder and said she wanted his gun."

"She said *what?*"

"Said she wanted his gun and held out her hand for it. The other hijacker was up front near the cockpit and you should have seen his face! For a second he was too surprised to do anything, and then he aimed his gun and pulled the trigger."

"At her?"

He nodded. "Yes, only instead of killing Miss Pym he killed his friend by mistake, because the other hijacker had turned—moved, you see—to look at Miss Pym."

"And that's when you jumped up and wrestled the surviving hijacker to the floor?" inquired the reporter.

The soldier nodded.

"And your name?"

"Staff Sergeant William Holliday, sir. But I couldn't have done it without her taking on the hijacker at *her* end of the plane." He looked at Amanda Pym admiringly.

"And you, Miss Pym—Amanda Pym, isn't it? You risked your life and saved the lives of two hundred and three passengers. Those men were threatening to shoot all of you, weren't they?"

Miss Pym nodded.

Farrell, frowning, said crossly, "This is the most unlikely heroine I've ever seen."

The interviewer was obviously struggling to capture a quote from her, to force her to say something, but she didn't respond. He said, "Well, I can tell you right now, Miss Pym, there's a car waiting for you"—he pointed—"to take you to a hotel where—"

The words were blotted out by a plane's landing in the distance.

"Watch closely now," said Carstairs.

The camera followed Amanda Pym as she was escorted to the exit and outside, accompanied by the cameraman and a swarm of interested onlookers. The camera zoomed in on several cars waiting, and the group paused. . . . A man stepped out of the nearest car; from the second car a man already stood with the rear door open. Amanda Pym walked to the second car, entered, and was swiftly driven away.

"And that," said Carstairs, "is the last anyone saw of Amanda Pym."

There was a startled silence, and then Mrs. Pollifax said, "She got into the wrong car . . . ?"

"Kidnapped in public view!" exclaimed Farrell. "I'm astonished."

Mrs. Pollifax was frowning. "I did see some of that television interview weeks ago, not all of it—I think I was cooking dinner at the time—but she surprised me even then. She was safe, she'd survived, she was being honored for her courage and she didn't show the slightest sign of being relieved or excited. In fact she had no personality at all."

"None whatsoever," agreed Carstairs. "An enigma."

"And yet think what she did," marveled Farrell. "But if the news was so big at the time, why was there nothing in the newspapers about her disappearance? Or was there?"

Carstairs said dryly, "Naturally it was assumed that Miss Pym would be wined and dined somewhere—by the airline or by our embassy—but when she couldn't be found at any hotel in the city the embassy thought it wise to issue a statement that she'd been taken to a hospital to be treated for nervous exhaustion." He shrugged. "And with no concerned parents or relatives—"

"None?" said Mrs. Pollifax.

"None . . . and thus the story died. Tactfully," he added, "because a member of our State Department was due to arrive the next day to once again discuss possible peace talks between Assad and Israel."

Farrell nodded. "Which al-Assad refuses to discuss unless Israel will consider returning the Golan Heights they took over after the Six-Day War in 1967."

"Yes," said Carstairs, "but to depart for the moment from the immediate, let me tell you what we *do* know. The two hijackers on the plane have been identified as members of a group called Crusaders of the Faith. At this particular time in history there are terrorist groups who get their training in Syria, groups that Assad is content to shelter, *possibly* arm, but allow to train while denying their existence. But we have no idea who the people were who abducted Miss Pym."

Puzzled, Mrs. Pollifax said, "But what I don't understand is how Farrell and I can possibly find a girl who disappeared in Syria, of all places, when nobody else could find her and neither of us speaks Arabic."

"You'll not be without help," said Carstairs.

"Help?"

Farrell gave Carstairs a keen glance. "May I ask by whom?"

"No," said Carstairs sharply.

This was interesting but Mrs. Pollifax had a question to ask. She said thoughtfully, "If the people who abducted Miss Pym happen to belong to the same group as the hijackers—these Crusaders of the Faith—this brings in the element of revenge, doesn't it? After all, Miss Pym interfered with *somebody's* plans: one hijacker killed, the other captured. She may have been killed minutes after being kidnapped."

"Oh yes," agreed Carstairs, "and frankly that's what both the embassy and the State Department believe . . . that she's dead. On the other hand," he added smoothly, "we have resources and sources the embassy in Damascus lacks, and that we don't always share with them."

"Such as?"

"Certain rumors have reached us," Carstairs said, "that Amanda Pym is still alive."

"Reliable rumors?" asked Mrs. Pollifax.

"Bazaar rumors but reliable."

"So that's why we're here," Farrell said, nodding.

"That's why you're here, yes. The two prevalent questions are, why there have been no demands for ransom, and—if revenge was behind her abduction—why it appears that she may still be alive. If she's alive we want to know how and why and where, and who abducted her, and who she is, and get her out of Syria. We feel it's far less provocative to send a woman who happens to be related to Miss Pym in some way." He added dryly, "More innocent, shall we say? Now hand over your passports so we can secure those visas. There are no direct flights to Syria from our country, so you'll fly early on Sunday to London and continue your trip on their Syrian Arab Airlines. We'll cable the embassy to reserve you rooms at the Cham Palace—adjoining rooms if they have them, so you can keep a firm eye on each other, since I'd prefer that neither of you be abducted. Anything else, Bishop?"

Bishop promptly said, "Plane tickets, passports, Syrian and U.S. money . . ."

"Oh yes, and a guidebook for each of you. They'll be delivered to each of you by courier no later than Saturday, along with hotel reservations and funds." He looked from Mrs. Pollifax to Farrell and frowned. "If I didn't believe you experienced enough, and qualified—" He stopped and said gruffly, "Just don't take any damn-fool risks."

Mrs. Pollifax smiled. *"Now* he tells us."

"I find it downright paternal of him," Farrell told her with a grin.

"So that's it," concluded Carstairs, "unless . . . any questions?"

"Yes," said Mrs. Pollifax quietly. "I think there's more to this, isn't there? You let slip the fact that you not only want to know if Amanda Pym is alive but also *who* she is."

Carstairs gave her a long look. "My mistake," he admitted. "It slipped out."

"Well?"

He was silent and then he said reluctantly, "We find ourselves very curious about this enigmatic Miss Pym. You saw her on film . . . it troubles us that we can learn almost nothing about her except for a few bare facts: she comes from a small Pennsylvania farming town, Roseville, population less than ten thousand . . . father owned a discount store and is dead, mother recently died, but no one in Roseville seems to have really known Amanda Pym. She's twenty-three years old but she seems to have moved through life not being noticed at all, just the sort of person who is susceptible and easily used. We've begun to wonder if Amanda could be more than she appears to be."

"What does that mean?" asked Farrell.

He hesitated and then, "It means that, incongruous as it may sound to you, it's occurred to us—cynics, skeptics, and doubters that we are—that this sullen young woman you saw on film might have deliberately entered the wrong car—which she did, without hesitating. Or to put it bluntly," he said, "we've wondered if she might have been expected."

A startled Mrs. Pollifax said, "You're not serious!"

"You really think that?" asked Farrell.

Carstairs sighed. "I have to remind you," he said patiently, "that we're neither a Traveler's Aid Society nor a lost-and-found department; we take no one and nothing for granted, and advise you to do the same. Whatever she may be, she's an American citizen and it's our responsibility to get her back. Just locate her if she's alive and the State Department can handle the rest. Unless, of course, you can bring her back yourselves."

With a glance at the clock on the wall he pushed back his chair and stood up. "I see that already I'm late for a conference Upstairs," he said dismissively, and with a tight smile he shook hands with each of them. "Bishop will see you out. Happy hunting, Godspeed and good luck," he added, and was gone.

"Well, *that* was abrupt," Farrell said to Bishop.

Bishop shrugged. "It happens. He's not as tough as people assume, you know, he worries." Especially, thought Bishop, when Emily Pollifax is concerned. No doubt Carstairs was suddenly remembering the nasty prisons in Syria: the Mezza in Damascus, for instance, and Tadmor just beyond the ruins of Palmyra, not to mention the fact that Mrs. Pollifax had returned from her last trip with a bullet freshly dug out of her arm. "It will pass," he lied.

"And so must I," said Mrs. Pollifax with a glance at her watch. "I believe there's a car waiting for me somewhere, and the plane you sent for me this morning." She rose. "See you Sunday, Farrell," she told him with a smile.

And having said good-bye she went home to reassure Cyrus that Syria was merely a reconnaissance trip, a matter of making inquiries about a missing young girl named Amanda.

2

Mrs. Pollifax arranged for Mrs. Lupacik to cook dinners for Cyrus while she was away; the two had already become friends when Cyrus had occupied the living room with a broken leg while Mrs. Pollifax, at the same time, had lain in bed upstairs with a particularly virulent case of flu. Mrs. Lupacik, she remembered, has also proven very educational for Cyrus, being an expert on the plot and history of every existing soap opera.

After canceling her karate lesson, and the talk she was to give at the Save Our Environment club, Mrs. Pollifax said her goodbyes, packed one suitcase and a carry-on bag, and at dawn met Farrell at Kennedy Airport.

"Cyrus pacified?" he asked sympathetically.

"Partially," she told him. "He's teaching law three days a week; he says he feels useful and is enjoying it very much, which is quite natural since, after all, that's *his* world."

Farrell nodded. "And this, my dear Duchess, admit it or not, is *your* world."

She smiled. "I would hate to admit that," she told him, "but it's certainly more useful than raising prizewinning geraniums. Do you think I'm addicted, Farrell?"

"We all are," he said cheerfully. "Why the hell else would we be here at dawn, prepared for another plunge into the unknown? Not to mention a long *long* flight ahead of us, and a stopover in London."

She sighed. *"Very* long—I remember," she acknowledged, and before boarding invested in six magazines.

It was late evening when Mrs. Pollifax and Farrell landed in Damascus. The plane from London had been delayed several hours due to fog, and when they disembarked it was to enter a dimly lit terminal almost deserted except for a few khaki-clad police leaning on rifles and observing the passengers with mild curiosity. Because of the fog and the delay there had been cancellations and the plane arrived half-filled; at Passport Control only one official was on duty, which led to a thirty-minute wait, after which, securing their luggage, they passed into the Arrivals hall. Here too there was the feel of late-hour desertions: the booths that would earlier have been manned by hotel representatives were mostly abandoned, leaving behind only bright signs describing the delights of the Cham Palace, the Meridien Hotel, the Sheraton, Semirames, and Umayyad.

As they approached the Information counter Farrell and Mrs. Pollifax were intercepted by a young man in tweed with a shock of red hair. "Pollifax and Farrell?" he asked.

"Sounds like a vaudeville team," said Farrell. "That's us, yes."

"Jacoby from the embassy," he told them, shaking hands. "Welcome to Syria, I've a car waiting."

"So kind of you," murmured Mrs. Pollifax, suppressing a desire to yawn.

With a brisk professional smile Jacoby said, "Since you are relatives of the late Miss Pym—"

Oh dear, thought Mrs. Pollifax, *late Miss Pym?*

"—we want to be of service to you in any way we can. We've scheduled a meeting for you—not in the morning; it's nearly Monday already, you'll want to rest, but Tuesday morning we'd like to go over with you everything we've done to find her. The ambassador will want to express his sympathy, too, if his schedule allows. You're a close relative of Miss Pym's?"

She exchanged an amused glance with Farrell. "Distant," she said.

"Aunt," put in Farrell firmly. "By distant she means she lived at a distance from, er, Amanda. No one," he added reproachfully, "notified her at all. Of her niece's disappearance."

"We did inquire," Jacoby said smoothly. "We did, you know. Here's my car, I'll put your luggage in the trunk." With this done he handed them into the car and took his place behind the wheel.

"But it's so *dark,*" said Mrs. Pollifax as they left the terminal behind. "Where are the lights?"

Over his shoulder Jacoby said, "This isn't America, you know. There aren't many lights

anywhere at night except in the center of
Damascus, although here and there on the
outskirts merchants wreath their shops with
strings of Christmas-tree lights—the pros-
perous ones who can afford it."

"But enough voltage along this airport
road to illumine picture after picture of President Assad," pointed out Farrell.

"Oh ´yes, you'll find him everywhere.
You've come, of course, needing closure on
her mysterious disappearance?"

Closure . . . what an odd word, thought
Mrs. Pollifax, as if anyone could slam a door
and say "It's over." It had a surgical sound
that grated.

Farrell said piously, "We'd like to recover
her body and bring her home."

"Oh I doubt that," Jacoby told them from
the front seat. "She's never been found, you
know."

This reduced them to silence; there was
really nothing left to say, Jacoby having
neatly disposed of Amanda Pym. It was a
long drive, and a dark one; Mrs. Pollifax's
impressions were of traffic circles, almost
no traffic, and the flat silhouette of the city
ahead, and since it was dark and she had
been traveling since dawn she found her

eyelids growing heavier and heavier. Presently she closed her eyes and fell asleep until the car came to a stop and she opened her eyes to the brilliant lights of a hotel.

"Here you are—the Cham Palace," Jacoby said. "I'll come in with you and see that you're registered."

"No," Farrell said sharply, and then, with an apologetic smile, added, "We can manage very well, thanks, you must be wanting your sleep, too. Thanks awfully."

"A bit rude but clever," suggested Mrs. Pollifax as they stood with their suitcases and watched Jacoby drive away. "And very necessary," she added, turning gratefully to the welcoming lights of the hotel. Entering through wide glass doors they walked into a bright lobby with a tiled fountain in its center, surrounded by comfortable lounging chairs and green trees rising out of large, square planters.

"Beautiful," she breathed. "Do you think our arrival's being noted?"

"Let's hope so—by *someone,*" Farrell said fiercely. "Carstairs did imply sources and resources—"

"But not what, who, when, or how," she put in.

"No, which leaves me feeling extraordinarily helpless at the moment, since we know absolutely no one here and Syria's a big country."

"In square miles, 71,498," she told him proudly. "Population twelve million people and fourteen governorates. I looked it up before we came."

"Twelve million people and we're looking for just one?" he growled.

"We can always be tourists if no help arrives."

"Don't depress me," he told her. "Let's register and get some sleep—you know, what 'knits the ravel'd sleeves of care'? Inspiration may arrive."

At Registration their passports were carefully examined while a man in a trench coat leaned easily against the counter some distance away. When they left, bearing keys to rooms 401 and 402, Mrs. Pollifax turned and saw the man in the trench coat move to the counter to examine their names. The elevator bore them to the fourth floor; their rooms were next to each other but there was no inside door between them.

"We'll have to pound on the wall if we want to talk," said Mrs. Pollifax with a sigh.

"Or phone?" suggested Farrell.

Mrs. Pollifax shook her head. "I think not. There was a man in the traditional trench coat watching as we registered."

"Ah, those damn trench coats," murmured Farrell.

"Except they don't always wear them," she reminded him. "Let's check the walls. You pound in your room, I'll pound in mine."

Once she had deposited her suitcase on the bed Mrs. Pollifax was tempted to laugh hysterically as she obediently pounded on her wall and was answered by a loud knock on the wall from room 402.

"Good," she murmured, and opening her suitcase extracted pajamas, cold cream, and a hairbrush and went into the bathroom for a quick shower before retiring for her first sleep since she'd left home. Returning to the bedroom she was startled to see a coarse sheet of paper lying just inside her door; it had not been there before.

Quickly she picked it up. In block letters she read: CITADEL IN SOUK OF INTEREST PLEASE AT 12 NOON MONDAY. DROP MAP ENCLOSED. Below these words was a primitive drawing of a square surrounded by alleys or streets with arrows pointing to an X, presumably the Citadel.

She knocked on Farrell's wall, hoping he'd not fallen asleep. There was no return knock on her wall; it came instead at her door, and she opened it to find Farrell there in a blindingly colorful Mexican serape.

"Come in," she whispered. "Anyone in the hall?"

"Not a soul," he whispered back and lifted one eyebrow questioningly until she handed him the note.

"Thank God," he murmured, and in a louder voice, "Then you suggest we meet for breakfast, say, at nine-thirty for some sight-seeing? Find a taxi, I suppose, unless that's too early for you?"

"Not at all," she told him. "Remember what they told us at the desk: dinners are on the sixth floor, breakfasts on the first floor."

He nodded. "First floor it is, then, at nine-thirty." And with a grin and a salute he returned to his room, each of them retiring for the night with an infinite sense of relief: Carstairs's sources and resources had found them.

3

Mrs. Pollifax was awakened only once, at dawn, by a distant muezzin's call to prayer drifting across the city; for a few minutes she lay in bed listening to the melodic *"Allâhu akbar, allâhu akbar, allâhu akbar . . ."* And then her eyes closed. When she awoke again dawn was an hour old and she felt well rested but very much suspended between two worlds, a dangerous way to feel in a new country if one was here to meet a stranger at noon who might have news of an Amanda Pym. As an antidote she practiced a few Yoga stretching exercises, reread the note left under her door the previous evening, and after this felt ready to begin what she suspected would be a very interesting day.

Before meeting Farrell for breakfast she

deliberately stopped in the lobby to make inquiries of the desk clerk. With a bright smile she said, "I need some advice."

"But of course," he said, returning her smile. "No problem."

"After breakfast," she emphasized, aware of the man leaning against the counter not far away, "I'll wish a taxi to take me to the souks." Holding up her guidebook she added, "This says the Citadel is in the top northwest corner of the Old City. That would be the best place to begin?"

Politely he leaned over to look at the small map. "Yes. You will want to see the Great Mosque, too, very near to it, but the Citadel is a good place to start. The taxi can stop you at the Souk Al Hamadye. You wish a guide?"

"Oh no, thank you. But a taxi, yes?"

He nodded. "When you have completed breakfast we will have taxi to wait. No problem."

She thanked him cordially and went downstairs to the room where long tables had been arranged for buffet breakfasts. There she found that Farrell had preceded her and had been captured by an enthusiastic young couple who were plainly American, too. As Mrs. Pollifax joined them with her tray of food the young woman said, "We were just telling your cousin how you *must* take a drive up Mount Qasiyun; you can see all of Damascus spread out below you and there are cafés, and fun rides for children, and on the way"—she lowered her voice—"on the way our tour driver said we passed what they call the 'security triangle,' quite hidden, where the president, Mr. Assad, lives. On the mountain, way above the Sheraton Hotel."

"And there's a mosque on top of the mountain, too," added her companion. "Going there certainly takes one above the smog, I might add. Finished, Becky?"

"Quite," she said, beaming at them both, and put down her cup of coffee. "So nice talking to you," she added. "We did the souks yesterday. Today . . ." She made a face. "Today the tour takes us to the museums."

When they had gone Farrell said with a lift of an eyebrow, "Well, Duchess?"

"There will be a taxi," she told him. "The Citadel being in the top corner of the map, it's nicely accessible. My inquiries were overheard, as expected . . . a short man with a mustache in a black suit."

Farrell nodded. "I was up early and went out for a walk. Very crowded city, Damascus, a hell of a lot of soldiers posted everywhere— I suppose it solves the unemployment problem—and quite a traffic jam, so much so there are actually bridges built over the roads for pedestrians to cross." He lifted his cup of coffee to his lips, and before sipping it added, "I was followed."

She nodded thoughtfully. "I think we are going to have to be *very* imaginative, ingenious and resourceful, Farrell. It's strange, because on the surface everything is so benign, so ordinary, but underneath . . ."

"Exactly."

She finished her egg, the cup of strong sweet coffee, and half of the unleavened bread they called *khobz,* dropping the other half into her purse for later. "Ready?"

He nodded. "Off we go, Duchess, but no Mount Qasiyun for us, alas."

They ascended in the elevator to the lobby, where the hotel clerk looked disconcerted to see that she was not alone, but, rallying, he smiled. "The taxi, yes?"

"Yes, thank you."

He gestured to a porter, who led them out of the lobby and past the tour buses to an ancient Studebaker painted bright yellow, parked and waiting. "There," he said. "Tak-see!" and to the driver, "Souk al Hamadye . . . la Citadelle!"

The driver leaped from the car to hold the door open for them, a broad-faced beaming man in a bright print sweater. *"Amerikâni,"* he said, tenderly helping Mrs. Pollifax into the rear seat. *"Aslan!* Welcome! My name is Abdul!"

"Shukren, Abdul," she told him cheerfully.

Once behind the wheel he shouted above the rattles of the car, "Me, I have cousin in"—he fumbled for the word—"Minapolis?"

"Minneapolis," she said. "Lovely city."

Farrell gave her an interested glance and she shrugged; certainly Minneapolis must be lovely, even though she'd never seen it. As they reached an intersection she nudged Farrell, discreetly pointing to the traffic policeman who was mounted on a high platform with what struck her as a charming black-and-white-striped miniskirt around its base. The car turned the corner with reckless abandon and Abdul said, "There is National Museum, you see?"

With a soldier and rifle, she noted.

"And that is army museum." Again he slowed to point.

Two khaki-clad soldiers on guard. "And the central post office." Again soldiers with rifles. "And now Martyrs' Square. Very busy this hour."

"What are they doing?" Farrell asked, peering from the window. "Tossing out cartons of cigarettes?"

Abdul shrugged. "From Lebanon, they come each morning to sell."

"Smuggled," whispered Farrell, and to Abdul, "And for whom is Martyrs' Square named?"

Abdul lifted both hands alarmingly from the wheel to shrug. "From many years back, you know? World War One." Mercifully he returned his hands to the steering wheel. "The Ottomans very cruel; they hang patriots here. But now you see the gate and walls of Old City? I leave you at entrance to the souks, you walk straight—past shops—and there will be Citadel."

He stopped the car, rushed to open doors for them and they shook hands with him, liberally tipping him, before he rattled off again in his Studebaker. "That car," said Farrell, watching him leave, "has to be held together by baling wire and prayers. But Carstairs was certainly right about people being friendly."

"Not everyone," commented Mrs. Pollifax. "Don't look now, but another car stopped behind Abdul, and there's a man in dark glasses and a black suit getting out."

"Tiresome," murmured Farrell. "If it's us he's interested in, we have . . ." He glanced at his watch. "We have a little less than two hours to lose him. The trick will be to lose *him,* but *not* our way back to the Citadel, because from the look of the map the Old City's a real maze."

"We could sprinkle bread crumbs as we go," said Mrs. Pollifax brightly. "Like Hansel and Gretel."

Farrell laughed. "If I remember *that* nursery tale the birds then ate all the crumbs, removing all possibility of their return. How's your sense of direction?"

"Only fair," she admitted.

"Well, mine's pretty well honed. Let's go."

"To be an authentic tourist I shall buy something," she told him. "Didn't it surprise you the amount of money Carstairs gave us?"

Farrell said dryly, "I'm not sure gifts were what he had in mind. Bribes, more likely. Baksheesh and all that."

She didn't question this, preferring not to, and in any case they were passing the ancient crumbling walls and entering old Damascus. They were also leaving behind the bright sunlight—it needed a moment for the eyes to adjust to the roofed passageways—but they exchanged sunshine for people, bright colors, the sound of shuffling feet on the cobbles, voices, and from somewhere there came music, a woman singing in Arabic, with guitars plucked and men chanting. "Wonderful," breathed Mrs. Pollifax.

"It would be *more* wonderful if we weren't being followed," growled Farrell.

She glanced back and sighed. "He does cling, doesn't he . . . if discreetly."

Ignoring him they gazed into stalls selling ice cream, tourist souvenirs, candy, and embroidered linens. Black-robed women passed them, and chattering schoolgirls in jeans and T-shirts, a man with a long white beard wearing a shabby djellaba, and everywhere merchants called out to them the pleasures of their merchandise.

Mrs. Pollifax abruptly stopped. "I must take a picture of this."

"You brought a *camera?*"

She nodded, smiling. "For Cyrus. I promised," and she snapped a picture of a counter piled high with tubs of dates, eggplants, figs, and cucumbers. The merchant beamed at her and called to her, " *'Berrid 'alâ kalbak!"* and she snapped a picture of him, too. Strolling on past several more stalls she stopped in midpassageway and put out a hand to halt Farrell, pointing. "That man sells clothes," she said. "I want a robe."

The attentive man behind the counter smiled. "For women, *galabiyyas* . . . very nice brocade, you like?"

"Oh no, a quiet one." She selected a richly woven black robe with embroidery, tried it on, and without bargaining paid his price. "Just in case I need to blend into the scenery," she told Farrell in a low voice, and looking him over critically added, "A pity you no longer have a mustache, you're tanned, enough to almost look a native." Turning back to the merchant she said, "And that white headscarf, please?"

"Isharb—kerchief," she was told, and he showed her how it could be intricately wound around her head to fall in soft folds. Once both purchases were wrapped in brown paper and string they walked on until it was Farrell who stopped. "Good-looking sharp knives," he said, fingering one. "How much? *Addaish?"*

"Just in case?" she said dryly.

"Gives one a bit of confidence," was all that he would say, pocketing it.

The narrow street of booths grew brighter, they saw light ahead and emerged in a broad square dominated by a large sand-colored building of intricately cut stones, surrounded by scaffolding.

"The Citadel," breathed Farrell, pointing to a sign that identified it and explained in Arabic, French, and English that it was being restored. "So—we've found it," said Farrell.

Mrs. Pollifax nodded. "Yes, but it's barely eleven o'clock and we can't stand here for an hour."

"Take a picture while I consult the guide-book," said Farrell, and brought out his copy. "There's a Street Called Straight rec-ommended—that seems to really be its name, and— What's the matter?"

"My camera, it's jammed. Do you know anything about cameras?"

He thrust the guidebook at her. "Look up how we get to the Street Called Straight, I'll see what I can do."

Mrs. Pollifax traced lines on the tiny map and announced, "We walk to the Great Mosque and turn down whatever street we find across from it. It says the Street Called Straight proceeds all the way to the East Gate, where it ends. If it really is straight, Farrell, we shouldn't get lost."

"How old is this camera?" demanded Farrell.

Mrs. Pollifax made a face. "Quite old."

He returned it to her with a shake of his head. "If it has gears, they're worn out. If it doesn't have gears I don't know what else is wrong but Cyrus is going to have to settle for postcards. Let's go, Duchess. On our way back to the Citadel—he's still wandering around behind us, isn't he?—we can detour into these smaller alleys and lose him."

"Which we must," she said, nodding, and regretfully put away the camera.

Once on the Street Called Straight she began to wish that she were a true tourist, for they passed exquisite silks, antique Turkish swords, Persian rugs, and tables inlaid with mother-of-pearl. "The Park Avenue of old Damascus," she said, but at 11:20 they left the street to shake off their surveillant, turning into narrow alleyways with interesting twists and turns. Quickening their steps they ducked into an alley crowded with people, took a quick left turn and then a right, and found refuge behind a rug hanging seductively outside a shop, where they had the pleasure of seeing their surveillant pass them. A minute later they ducked out and retraced their steps. Once the Citadel was in sight they hung back until five minutes to the hour, and then strolled out into the square to stand conspicuously in front of the Citadel while Farrell ostentatiously examined their guidebook.

"No watchdog in sight," she reported uneasily. "I believe we lost him. Not many people here either."

A small group of tourists, not far away, surrounded a guide, listening to his lecture. A pair of women in dark robes and headscarves walked past them. With a glance at her watch Mrs. Pollifax dropped the map to the ground. A boy of nine or ten in a bright red sweater passed the tourists, and as he strolled toward them glanced down at the map. Before she could stop him he politely bent over to pick it up, fumbled with it for a moment and handed it to her. *"Khud,* madam," he said with a smile and a small bow.

But he had returned to her not only the map but a slip of paper with the printed words: FOLLOW BOY, NOT FAST.

Mrs. Pollifax reached into her pocket for a coin—an American fifty-cent piece—and gave it to him. *"Shukren,"* she said gravely and handed Farrell both the map and the note. "We go," she said. "But slowly."

"Thank heaven," said Farrell.

Casually they strolled toward the same alley down which the boy had gone, his red sweater still in sight but at a distance. Seeing him turn left they quickened their pace, passing displays of water pipes, followed by a shop with children's bright clothes hanging from rods. The boy had turned again, this time to the right, and they hurried lest they lose him in this labyrinth of stalls. They needn't have worried. The boy paused at a souk displaying carpets of all kinds; he lingered only for a moment and then without looking back he slipped down a narrow brick-lined passage next to the rug stall. Following, they saw him open a handsome door of mahogany and disappear, leaving the door ajar.

"Here we go," whispered Mrs. Pollifax, and took a deep breath.

Pushing the door open and closing it behind them they found themselves in a store-room occupied by a desk piled high with papers and surrounded by roll upon roll of kilim and Oriental rugs standing upright, like sentinels. A particularly fine Oriental rug that hung from the far wall caught Mrs. Pollifax's eye, and as she stepped closer to admire it a hand appeared, the carpet was drawn aside, and a man stepped out. He wore a voluminous striped robe and a checkered kaffiyeh wrapped around his head and bound with a cord; he also wore sunglasses and a pointed beard so that in the dimness of the room it was impossible to see the features of his face clearly. Only the whiteness of his teeth penetrated the shadows as he smiled and bowed. *"As salaam alaikum."*

Mrs. Pollifax, remembering her adventures in Jordan, smiled and said, *"Alaikum as salaam."*

There was the flash of white teeth again. In clipped English he said, "And how is your health?"

"Well, thank God . . . but have you news?"

"There is news, yes." The boy in the red sweater suddenly reappeared, bearing a tray with tiny glasses of tea. "Please," said their host, gesturing them toward chairs dimly discerned near the desk. "You may call me Omar if you wish."

Cups in hand they obediently sat down. Examining each of their faces Omar said, "You know you are being watched. From the moment your plane landed you have been followed."

"That soon?" Farrell said, frowning. "We were expected?"

Gravely the man said, "The American Embassy here has many leaks. They employ cooks, interpreters, cleaners, workmen, all Syrian." He shrugged. "But the boy Abdul is well trained and you can be sure you were not followed to me here. By now, of course, they will have learned you look for a missing young woman—"

Mrs. Pollifax interrupted him to say, "Yes, but there *is* news of her? She is alive?"

"There are rumors. . . ."

"Such as?" asked Farrell.

Omar lifted a cup of tea to his lips, blotted his lips with a napkin and replaced the cup on the tray. "Of a young woman, presumably American, in a place where no American woman should be. We hear of this because of a Bedouin whose sheep had strayed, and in his wanderings—what he saw and heard he mentioned to a friend, who spoke of it to another man who is interested in such matters."

You, thought Mrs. Pollifax but did not say so.

"It was some time ago, you understand. It needed many days for news of this to pass from person to person—and there are distances. . . ."

"We're here to investigate the rumor," said Farrell. "This is the aunt"—he gestured toward Mrs. Pollifax—"of the young American who disappeared."

"Really?" he said, amused.

"And the embassy appears to have heard nothing of this rumor."

"Oh, they would not hear of it, no," the man said smoothly.

"But go on, please," said Mrs. Pollifax.

"May I ask how a Bedouin looking for his sheep would know this young woman was American? And how can we find him?"

"It is you who will have to find him," he said. "Do drink your tea, it has a delicious jasmine flavor, I assure you. As for the Bedouin I can only tell you what was told to me by . . . a friend," he emphasized. "In the desert there are no—what can I say?— no water closets, no lavatories, no privies? It was night but there was a moon, and in his search for his missing sheep this man heard voices, he was curious, and kneeling behind a small hill of stones he saw the shape of two people answering . . . shall we say the call of nature? He heard one—a woman—say, *'Dir balak, wuisikh Amerikâni!'* which, translated, means, 'Pay attention, dirty American.'

"The second young woman," he continued, "—the 'dirty American'—spat a word at her companion the Bedouin did not know, after which her companion said angrily, *'Khanzir, wusikh Amerikâni?'* "

"Meaning?" asked Farrell.

"Meaning, *'Pig,* you dirty American?' The so-called dirty American shouted *'Aiwa'*— meaning yes," he added, "and they began to fight, pulling each other's hair and rolling on the ground. The Bedouin left, astonished by such violence and finding it very strange an American was there. So much I have heard, no more."

"But where was this?" asked Mrs. Pollifax. "Where can we find this Bedouin?"

He shrugged. "Where sheep go astray and Bedu search. I have been . . . shall we say asked to help you in this small manner, but if it is a question of actually finding this woman . . ."

"It's why we are here," Farrell told him flatly.

"Then I can only . . . Let me think."

They waited patiently for several minutes.

"Tomorrow," he said abruptly, "you must be the tourists and visit Palmyra, which is several hours to the north—our famous ruins—while I make contact—" He stopped. "Let me consider." After another silence he said, "At some point while you admire the ruins a man will speak to you. It is he who will know at what camp the Bedouin stopped for water and spoke of this American. He will know in what direction you must go, and he will know also the name of the Bedouin who heard this in the night, and which I do not know. Or want to know," he added firmly.

"Palmyra," repeated Mrs. Pollifax.

"Its original name is Tadmor and the town is Tadmor; the ruins are Palmyra. You will need the morning to drive there, it's three hours from Damascus. Let's say between one and two o'clock in the afternoon you will be approached."

"How will we know it's not just someone who wants to talk to Americans?" asked Mrs. Pollifax.

"There could be that," he said thoughtfully. "Then I would suggest . . ." He sounded amused. "Suggest you work into your conversation the word *sheep*." He added dryly, "How you do that I will leave to you. And now if you'll excuse me . . ."

"Yes, of course," said Farrell, putting down his cup.

As if by magic the boy Abdul appeared, this time in a black T-shirt, and Mrs. Pollifax said warmly, "We thank you very much."

He ignored this. "Do not follow too closely. When you no longer see him you will be near enough to the Citadel to find your own way."

The heavy door was opened, they were

gestured to leave first, and once they had negotiated their return to the narrow street outside the boy passed them, sauntering slowly on ahead of them, his hands in his pockets. His route was certainly circuitous. "So we can never know where we've been," pointed out Farrell.

"On the contrary," said Mrs. Pollifax demurely, "like Hansel and Gretel I noted that before we turned the corner we passed a barbershop, a souk that sold sheepskins, another selling copper pots, and two very large photos of President Assad, one smiling and one serious."

Five minutes later the boy vanished completely from sight.

4

They spent the remainder of Monday in finding a way to get to Palmyra the next morning. They did not want the company of a
guide for the entire day. Buses needed reservations a day in advance, and the possibility of service taxis sounded doubtful.
Eventually they concluded their research by
arranging, through the hotel, a one-way
Transtour car with driver, an overnight at a
hotel in Tadmor, and a reservation for a similar car to return them to Damascus in the
morning.

And since the next day would be Tuesday
there was a note handed to them at the desk
from the embassy, inviting them to discuss
pertinent matters Tuesday morning at
eleven o'clock.

"I wonder what they'd tell us," mused

Mrs. Pollifax, tearing up the note. "I shall retire early with my broken camera and guidebook and catch up on sleep. You can carouse if you'd like," she kindly told Farrell.

"Carouse?" he said with amusement. "My dear Duchess, having inched past the age of forty, and following a fourteen-hour flight, I have to confess sleep has enormous appeal to me, too."

Their driver the next morning was an affable young man named Khalid. He spoke English "and much French, too," he announced with a flashing smile, and he had been trained for guiding tour groups, "But not many Americans yet," he added regretfully. "They say bad things about us that make us very sad. So far only three American groups for me over the summer." Having divested himself of this he began to fling cheerful comments over his shoulder as they started their drive to Palmyra, while Farrell glanced behind to see if they were being followed. *"Bilad-es-Sham,"* he said, was the Arab name for Syria, and once Damascus was a famous and beautiful oasis— "very green," he assured them, "very green and sweet in a country so much desert. And please," he said, "if you wish a picture with camera anytime, I will stop."

"Unfortunately," Mrs. Pollifax told him, "my camera broke in Damascus. No more pictures."

"Broke? Is *broken?*" he said in horror, as if a tourist without a camera was unthinkable. "In Tadmor there are Konic shops." He briefly turned his head to give them a happy smile. "With your permission we stop there, there may be a fresh camera for you."

"Gray car," said Farrell, having just glanced back at the road behind them. "Up to you, Duchess."

"If we could . . . Cyrus knows so much more history than I do that I know he'd appreciate some snapshots of Palmyra," and to Khalid, "If there is time . . . yes!"

"Good," he said, and continued his over-the-shoulder remarks as they passed through the modest industrial section of the city. "Business!" he said, nodding toward a factory and shaking his head. "Exporting goods no problem, but to import—*ya rabb!*—many snarls and troubles."

"Very old cars," commented Farrell. "But you have oil."

Khalid chuckled. "Before 1981 the oil in Syria's earth was heavy, not rich, but there was an underground earthquake in the eighties that changed it." He laughed. "We think oil flowed in from Iraq—good light oil suddenly!"

They were reaching the desert now, flat, tawny sand with tufts of grass, soon turning into pebbles and stones, a barren landscape except for a hazy blue mountain at a distance off to their left, and the great arc of blue sky overhead.

"Soon Tadmor," said Khalid.

"Palmyra or Tadmor?" asked Mrs. Pollifax, puzzled.

"Ah, the town she has always been Tadmor. Once it was called the City of Dates—you will see. But Palmyra—the Romans named it City of Palms—but no palms," he added humorously. "Now what is your hotel?"

"The Zenobia," said Farrell.

He nodded vigorously. "Good place, inside the town and inside Palmyra ruins also, you can walk with ease. The town has beautiful dates to sell; on your evening stroll you may find good Bedouin weavings, too, they bring them into Tadmor from the desert, but first we find you camera, yes?"

Reaching Tadmor, Khalid turned down a cobbled street lined with colorful signs. They passed an open market hung with huge clusters of dates, yellow, dark red, brown and black, and Mrs. Pollifax wished she could take a picture of this, and of the street, which had all the flavor of the Middle East.

Khalid stopped the car in front of a Konic sign. "I go with you," he said. "He may not speak such good English as me." They walked through the door into a dusty shop with lines of kerosene tins stacked along one wall, an ancient rifle suspended from the ceiling, an assortment of dull brass and copper pots, cases of cola, and glass jars and boxes on the shelves. A man shuffled out from an inner room, his lined brown face brightening at sight of them.

"Cameras?" he said. *"Yes!"* he exclaimed, and walking over to a wooden chest he opened it and delved into it, dug deep, and brought up a huge, dusty, forlorn-looking black box, and then another one equally as dusty and old. "Cameras," he said proudly. "Russkies."

"Russkies?" Farrell said in astonishment, touching one. "You mean these are *Russian* cameras?"

He nodded and announced that he would sell the somewhat smaller one for fifty American dollars, the larger for seventy-five.

"One could scarcely sling one of these over one's shoulder," said Mrs. Pollifax, looking at them with interest. "Or find film for them, either; they must be at least fifty years old."

"You buy?"

"*Shukren,* but no—*la,*" she said. "I'm sorry."

Khalid, embarrassed, said, "Perhaps another shop?"

Farrell intervened gently. "I think we'd better go on now to our hotel." Secretly he was wondering, with considerable amusement, what their surveillants must be making of this; as they left the shop he saw the familiar gray car parked discreetly at some distance up the street.

For a mere overnight stay Farrell had piled his gear into a knapsack, while Mrs. Pollifax had packed what she needed in an open straw bag with handles, into which she had added her new djellaba—or *galabiyyas,* as the merchant had called it—for the warmth of it at night. Finding a group of German tourists lined up at the hotel's registration desk, and knowing they already had a reservation, they were delighted to find a terrace that overlooked the ruins of Palmyra and where they could wait for the group to disperse. They retreated there at once, bags in hand, although not before Mrs. Pollifax had seized upon a copy of *Palmyra: History, Monuments & Museum*—"just what Cyrus will enjoy," she told Farrell. Once they were settled Farrell disappeared and returned with two plates of baba ghannoj, a beer and a cola, and they ate lunch gazing out upon the remains of the long-ago city that had been Palmyra, reduced now to acres of truncated columns, arches, walls and temples, the earth littered with fallen blocks of stone.

"Cyrus told me something of this," she mused. "Palmyra is where Queen Zenobia ruled, much loved and very successful until— Such a musical name, isn't it?"

"Until what?" asked Farrell, chasing the last shred of eggplant with a slice of bread.

"Until what I don't remember, except that eventually she was captured by the Romans and taken back to Rome to be paraded in gold chains."

"And now has a hotel named for her." Farrell nodded. "Such is immortality."

"Cynic," she retorted, and turned to her guidebook for directions. Their hotel stood just inside the walls of Palmyra, very near the streets of Tadmor. She said, "It looks as if we need only leave the hotel, turn to the right, and walk down the road past what's called the Temple of Baalshamin to reach the Monumental Arch that stands at the end of the main avenue." With a glance at Farrell she added, "We'd better go now; the noon call to prayer ended ten or fifteen minutes ago, we'll be late if we don't stir ourselves, register, and leave."

"I know." Farrell sighed. "It looks very hot down there and it's so comfortable here, although I admit I'm growing slightly tired of eggplant."

"Any sign of our not-so-friendly escorts?" she asked.

He nodded. "One man, dark glasses, was standing in the lobby looking very awkward and out of place. Okay, I'm up—but let's register later."

They strolled past the Temple of Baal-shamin, a portion of it remarkably well pre-served, and reaching the Monumental Arch Mrs. Pollifax brought out her Palmyra guide-book. "Third century A.D." she murmured.

"Not much left of it," commented Farrell.

Gazing up at the arch Mrs. Pollifax touched the rough-hewn blocks of stone. "Amazing that it still stands," she said. "Be-hind it are only a few columns, no roof, a litter of fallen stones but the arch remains."

A man who was passing overheard her words and paused—a handsome man in a striped black-and-white djellaba, his face narrow, ascetic, perhaps that of a scholar. A good face, thought Mrs. Pollifax. "There have been earthquakes, too, you see, as well as the years," he said in a friendly voice. He was holding the same guidebook on Palmyra that she carried, and he walked closer to show it to them.

"We see not Americans often. Mine too is in English, I work to learn." Leaning closer he said in a low voice, "Please note the page open."

Startled, they each stared blankly at the

picture of a castle fronted with stout round columns, under which were printed the words *The Eastern Qasr al-Hirt.* Farrell's eyes suddenly narrowed and he gave the man an interested look. "There is no castle like that at Palmyra, is there?"

The man smiled pleasantly. "Oh no. In English miles it is eighty miles to the east, well off the highway to Deir Ez Zor. You will see many *sheep* along the way."

"Sheep," murmured Mrs. Pollifax. "Yes— yes, we understand." The picture was on page 118, she noted, and she leafed through her book until she reached page 118 in her own Palmyra guide. "And you recommend it . . . ?"

He shrugged. "Only for its direction. It is known . . . there is a sign on highway announcing the Qasr in English and Arabic. But you do not go there. You stop, but do not go there. You cross the highway to a track leading south into the desert—direct south—where in ten miles there is a pot-hunting camp and—"

"Pot hunters? You mean archaeologists?" asked Farrell, frowning. "Digs?"

"Digs, yes. There may even be a small sign still planted in the earth there, with arrow. No road but track is clear—trucks go with supplies to them. Tell Khamseh—or Camp Five, in English. It is at this camp a Bedouin named Bazir Mamoul spoke of certain things he had seen. Bazir Mamoul," he repeated. "And you head to Qasr al-Hirt *east,*" he emphasized. "There is also a Qasr al-Hirt West—*no!*" He closed his book, saying, "It has been most interesting speaking with you."

With a smile he walked on, book in hand, as if studying it, and Farrell and Mrs. Pollifax quickly returned to an examination of the arch, pretending to share and study both the monument and the guidebook with renewed interest. After several minutes Farrell said, "We can't stand here forever."

"No, but I'm in shock," admitted Mrs. Pollifax. "We have to travel eighty miles to this castle and then out into the desert to find an archaeology camp?"

"I know. He didn't say *how,* only where."

Rallying, Mrs. Pollifax said, "And we never assumed it would be easy. One must be allowed, I suppose, a moment or two of *un*easiness. But I trusted him, didn't you?"

"Yes, and liked him," agreed Farrell.

They began strolling down the colon-

naded main avenue toward the theater, surrounded by single pillars rising like spears
above rubble and crumbling temples. With
a sigh—for Mrs. Pollifax preferred people to
monuments—she consulted her guidebook
again. "Hadrian was here," she announced.

"And Zenobia," teased Farrell.

"A pity she lived so long ago, you'd really
appreciate her, Farrell. It says here that she
had 'pale skin, black eyes and beautiful
teeth, white as pearls, and was considered
the most noble and most beautiful of all
women in the Orient.' " She closed the
guidebook. "Farrell, I don't feel like seeing
any more of Palmyra, we've got to make
plans. Find someone to drive us—or a bus—
and leave tomorrow for that archaeological
site."

Farrell nodded, and taking her by the arm
turned her around. "A bit strange to leave
such a world-renowned place so quickly,
but . . . we've established that we're not being followed, haven't we?"

"Yes, they're probably waiting for us at
the entrance," she said. "Or certainly by the
hotel, bored by following people around the
ruins. Now how do we get back to the hotel?"

"Return to the Monumental Arch and turn left, except . . ." He frowned. "Something seems to be happening down there, Duchess. By the Arch."

She had noticed it, too. A number of tourists had arrived and she had the impression of interrupted calm, of groups of people dissolving, re-forming and hurrying toward an undefined point where others had already collected; there were sounds of exclamations and a sudden scream. She and Farrell began to run, anxious to see what had claimed so many people; a museum guard in uniform had arrived to hold people back but Mrs. Pollifax pressed her way through, with Farrell elbowing people out of the way.

The crowd had formed a circle around a man who had fallen to the ground. Two khaki-clad soldiers had laid aside their rifles to bend over him, and as they straightened, Mrs. Pollifax gasped as she saw that the man on the ground wore a black-and-white striped robe and there was a spreading stain of red across his back. One of the men shrugged. *"Battâl,"* he said. *"Isbital!"* And leaning over the man he grasped his shoulders while his companion grasped his feet.

And for just a moment the man's face could be seen.

"Oh dear God," said Mrs. Pollifax. "Farrell—"

"Yes," he said grimly. "It's our friend. The same man. Our contact."

5

They were lifting the man with care. *"Excusez-moi,"* said the guard in French, and as the crowd parted, "Accident—*faire mal!"*

His companion, in Arabic, shouted, *"Intabeh! Hakeem!"*

Farrell said firmly, "Let's go. Don't look back, Duchess, let's *go*—and fast!"

"But *not* to the hotel," she gasped. "Not to the hotel, Farrell. Did you see the blood? Is he dead?"

"I saw it," he said bitterly. "And I don't mean to sound unfeeling, but for the moment we have to wonder if he was seen talking to us, poor chap. Where did Khalid say the bus station is? We've got to get out of here—and on the double!"

"He said it's a block beyond the post office in Tadmor, not far from the hotel. In case we wanted to mail postcards," she added dryly, trying to walk as fast as Farrell. "Farrell, slow down, we're tourists, remember?"

"Hah," was his only response but he slowed his pace. "What's the word for post office? I don't even speak French."

"Oh, *must* we ask the way?"

They had vanished down a road behind their hotel, and reaching the wall that surrounded Palmyra they turned back to the street leading into the town. "And there's the post office," said Mrs. Pollifax in relief. "The bus station must be just beyond it."

Farrell shook his head. "I think first we duck down a side street or two and make sure that chap in dark glasses hasn't caught up with us. Let's try this one."

They plunged down an alley, turning left and then right until they found themselves in the older section of town with its shabby restaurants, food stalls and shops. "In here," Farrell said, pointing to an even narrower alley between food stalls.

It was deeply shadowed, like a tunnel with brilliant light at either end; they stopped in midpassage and waited to see if they'd been noticed. At the far end, from which they'd entered, people walked past without interest or pause; the sounds of traffic and music filtered down to them, a child cried, and then two men in djellabas turned into the alley, busily talking to each other with gestures; one of them laughed and nodded.

"Pretend we're lost; I'll ask for the bus station," said Farrell. "We must look like fools standing here." He moved aside for them to pass.

Suddenly Mrs. Pollifax said, "Farrell, *no* . . . !"

It was too late. One man had seized Farrell's wrists and was tying a rope around them while the other man had stuffed a rag into Farrell's mouth and was placing a bag over his head. Shocked and furious, outnumbered and too late for karate, Mrs. Pollifax flung herself at the two men and in turn was hit over the head and sent reeling across the stone-paved alley to the ground.

She lay there, stunned from the fall, blood running into her eyes and blinding her. When at last she rallied and forced herself to sit up the alley was empty; Farrell was gone. Gingerly she checked arms and legs; no bones had been broken but she felt bruised all over from the force of the fall, one arm had been scraped raw from the sharpness of the stones and her head throbbed. Reaching a hand to her forehead she met with a flap of loose skin from which the blood was flowing. Blindly she reached out and found her purse beside her; she could at least be grateful they'd not taken her passport and money but her mind felt numbed by shock. She couldn't think, she could only begin to crawl toward the bright and empty end of the alley, to get out and away lest they come back for her, wanting no more than to leave this dark place of violence—yes, and of loss, for she'd lost Farrell. Near the end of the alley she stood up, unsteadily and dizzily, and by clinging to the wall made her way step by step out of the alley to find herself blinded by sun.

Blinking at the brightness, she saw ahead of her a long line of cement-block houses with balconies—people lived here—and nearest her a woman in a white headscarf was hanging towels and robes over the wall of her balcony.

Mrs. Pollifax stumbled toward her into the street and looked up at her. "Please?" she whispered, and then, louder, "Please? *Amerikâni?*"

The woman, seeing her, looked frightened

and then, after glancing up and down the street she gave a quick nod and vanished. An endless minute passed before the door to the street was opened; again the woman glanced up and down the street and then she rushed to Mrs. Pollifax, still looking from left to right, gasped, *"Yalla! Yalla!"* and half dragged, half carried her through the door and into the house. There she was placed on the floor—this blessed woman, thought Mrs. Pollifax—while the woman caught her breath and stared down at her until Mrs. Pollifax whispered, *"Shukren—*thank you!"

With this the woman suddenly smiled, nodded, and hurried away again, returning with a cloth dripping with water to wipe the blood from Mrs. Pollifax's temple. *Brave,* thought Mrs. Pollifax, remembering her anxious glances up and down the street. *"Shukren,"* she murmured again, and fainted.

When she opened her eyes she was lying on a mattress in a dim room, with the woman and a boy of twelve or thirteen looking down at her. The boy said, "I speak a small English, a wound has happened?"

Mrs. Pollifax lifted a hand to her forehead and winced. Impossible to explain, she thought, and said, "A rock . . . loose from the wall . . . fell. On me."

Whether they accepted this or not the woman spoke to the boy, who went into another room and returned with a tiny glass cup with pink roses on it.

"Kahweh," said the woman.

"Coffee," said the boy proudly, in English.

Mrs. Pollifax sat up and sipped it; it was strong and flavored with cardamom and it revived her enough to say to the boy, "Please thank your mother, she is so kind to take me into your house."

"Is okay," he told her. "She say rest." He frowned, thinking. "Until *aswad*—no, dark— you go. But do not go near windows."

"No," she said, and then again, *"Shukren,"* and struggled to sit up, knowing that she must or she'd never be able to leave. She was helped into a small living room crowded with furniture: cabinets, chairs, a sofa, pictures on the wall, a television set, plastic curtains at the windows. The television set was turned on, showing American cartoons with subtitles in Arabic. Thank heaven she still had her purse, she remembered, with aspirin in it as well as her passport and money. She opened it and managed to choke down three aspirin without water and reassured the boy, saying, *"Naam,* I rest until dark."

"Where, please, you go?" he asked.

At this she closed her eyes, feigning sleep because she didn't know how to answer him. It was time to think, and to think hard, to remind herself that Farrell, wherever he was, and whatever he was enduring, was more professional than she could ever be, and would somehow deal with it. She had to weigh her own possibilities and choices now. There was no American Embassy in Tadmor, and no one to whom she could appeal without becoming conspicuous. It was time to admit that the *mukhabarat* had outwitted them; they must have realized their surveillance was noticed, and they had cleverly removed their trench coats and dark glasses and donned djellabas and kaffiyehs instead, to haul Farrell off to the police station and interrogate him. Not at once, she thought forlornly, no, not at once . . . this was not a country where human rights were honored, but she had to forget Farrell for the moment, he would want her to; they had faced both death and captivity together in earlier times and she knew his courage and his resourcefulness. If, with luck, he could talk his way out of arrest and imprisonment there were only two places to find her again: either at the hotel in Damascus, or at the archaeological camp that lay to the south of the Qasr al-Hirt east, and she had no interest in returning defeated to Damascus.

He would know this, she thought. It was what Carstairs had asked of them, and they had a name and a destination now.

Her headache was subsiding and she'd stopped shivering from shock; touching her forehead she found the woman had placed a bandage over it. She would soon stand up and try to walk.

Presently the woman walked quietly into the room and placed something beside her, and opening her eyes Mrs. Pollifax saw that she was carrying her straw carry-on bag that had dropped in the alley when she fell. She sat up, surprised, and looked questioningly at the woman, who only smiled and nodded. The boy followed her into the room. He said, "She see it there. Is yours?"

Mrs. Pollifax nodded, and said, "How do I leave when . . . when *aswan*—dark?"

"Where, please, to go?" asked the boy. " *'Ala otel?*"

From the pocket of her jacket Mrs. Pollifax drew out her guidebook to Palmyra, found page 118 and tore it out. "The eastern Qasr al-Hirt," she told him, and pointed.

The boy looked at the picture and then at her, bewildered. "There is nothing there but rocks. Old—what do you say, antiquities?"

"But not far from it," said Mrs. Pollifax hopefully, "there is a—do you know the word *tell?* Where men dig? Dig up ruins? Antiquities?"

"Ah . . ." he murmured, nodding. *"Naam,"* and he explained to his mother what she had said.

His mother looked shocked and spoke quick words to her son, who looked at Mrs. Pollifax. "No man? *Kultu?* Man?"

She understood at once that a woman alone, even American, was looked upon with either great pity or much suspicion here. She would have to manufacture a son waiting for her at the archaeological camp; she remembered the name for mother was *umm* but she had to search her memory for the word son. At last, *"Ibn!"* she said triumphantly, and held up the picture again with her destination.

"Ahh . . ." murmured the woman, smiling and nodding. *"Ibn, naam,"* and glancing at her son spoke to him rapidly in Arabic.

He nodded eagerly. To Mrs. Pollifax he said, "My cousin go to . . ." He scowled, searching for the word, and disappearing into another room he returned with a small book. Running through the pages he said, "Delivers! Delivers!" and turning pages added, "Kerosene, chickens, lamb, beer."

"Where?" asked Mrs. Pollifax quickly.

"To As Sikhneh." He rubbed two fingers together. "With a little money he go more miles to digging place."

A flood of relief nearly overwhelmed her; this meant no taxi, no struggle to find a bus. "When does he go?" she asked.

"Tonight. After . . ." Again the shuffling of pages. "After work. In market."

Wonderful, she thought, it would be dark. "Can you tell him about me? And for money . . ." She also rubbed two fingers together. "For money I go with him?" She rummaged through her purse and brought out Syrian pound notes, handing them to him.

The boy counted them, beamed at her, and returned half of them to her. "Good. This money for now to Salim. Other half later. I go now to Salim, okay?"

Mrs. Pollifax thought it very okay, and when he had left she beckoned to the woman to stay with her for a moment and from her straw bag drew out the embroidered black djellaba for which she had probably paid as much as this woman saw in a week. Fumbling for her Arabic phrase book she thumbed through it. *"Hadeeya—gift,"* she told her, presenting it to her.

Astonished, she said with a gasp, *"Hilwah!"*

Mrs. Pollifax stood up and helped to lift it over her shabby long dress. *"Hilwah,* yes," she said, beaming at her. "On you, beautiful!"

But she would keep the long white headscarf, and she wound it around her head.

"Shukren, shukren," said the woman happily. *"Shawarma—*sandweech? Eat?"

The boy returned to say that Salim would stop in front of the house at *saba'a—*seven, when dark—and she must be ready. "And," he added triumphantly, "with money he will go to digging camp for you."

Mrs. Pollifax sighed with relief and once

again thanked them, after which the three of them sat companionably at the table in the kitchen and ate *shawarma,* drank cola, and waited for seven o'clock, and Salim.

6

At seven o'clock they waited for Salim just inside the door, and when they heard a truck stop outside the house the woman opened the door, examined the shape of the vehicle and then, nodding, led Mrs. Pollifax out to help her up into the seat beside the driver. No words were said, and Salim did not even glance at her; she might have been simply one of the tins and crates piled high in the rear of his truck. In the dim light of the dashboard his face was thin and swarthy, made darker by the snow white kaffiyeh that covered his head. His brows were thick and his mustache so luxurious that Mrs. Pollifax thought it must surely drain energy from such a thin and wiry body. There was neither smile nor greeting: Salim was a man in a hurry, a man, too, who must have worked hard all day in the market since dawn.

But to Mrs. Pollifax he was an angel.

He put the truck into gear and they were abruptly off down mean streets, heading out of town toward the desert and to As Sikhneh—or so she hoped, but she had to trust this man. It was twilight but a pale moon softened the shapes of old houses and crumbling walls, and as they left Tadmor behind for the emptiness of land flat to the horizon she admitted relief when she saw a sign announcing this was the highway to Deir Ez Zor, for the man at Palmyra—their ill-fated contact—had mentioned the highway to Deir Ez Zor.

He stopped the truck once, a stop that alarmed Mrs. Pollifax until she saw that because it was almost dark he had stepped several feet away from the truck, and after scrubbing his hands in the sand he faced east and sank to his knees. The moon and Mecca, she thought, nodding.

When he returned to the truck she said, "The Ashâ?"

For the first time he looked at her. "You know?" he said in surprised English.

She nodded.

"Taib," he said; she had become a human being to him suddenly, no longer a load to deliver.

After this Mrs. Pollifax fell asleep, much needed, a comforting sleep, too, soothed by the knowledge that through a succession of miracles she had met with help in this country of surveillants and fear; her errand for Carstairs had not been aborted after all.

She opened her eyes when they reached the lights of the desert town of As Sikhneh and the truck came to a halt. It was dark now and the moon was high in the sky. Men's voices were heard as Salim's truck was unloaded, she was aware of—restaurants? warehouses?—and then Salim returned to the truck and once out of town he stopped.

"Wein?" he asked. "Where?"

She thought it had been explained to him by the boy, but, fumbling for the pocket flashlight in her purse she drew out the photograph of Qasr al-Hirt and showed it to him, and then with a pencil marked an X and drew a line south into the desert. "Tell Khamseh?" Bringing out her Arabic dictionary, *"Hâjora?* Stones?" and made the motion of digging.

"Ah . . . Khamseh!" He nodded and with a shrewd glance at her held out his hand, ostensibly for more money.

Again consulting her dictionary she said apologetically, *"Ba 'dein.* Later?" and at once felt guilt at not completely trusting him, but it was late, it was dark, and she desperately wished to be delivered to the right place, not abandoned on the road in some strange town.

He accepted this. He could have wrested the money from her, she realized—really she was being foolish—but now that she was awake the cut on her forehead was throbbing again, and she yearned for more sleep. "My *ibn,"* she told him. "My son," and hoped that he thought her nonexistent son would pay him on arrival.

The unloading of food in As Sikhneh had taken time; it was past ten o'clock when they reached the sign directing the passerby down a road thirty kilometers to the Qasr al-Hirt. Here Salim left the truck to look for a path or track leading to the south and when he returned he was smiling cheerfully. *"Mashallah!* You did not say near al-Kom." He pointed south. "A small village on the wadi. I know now what place you seek."

"Allah be praised," she told him with a smile.

"Your son dig at camp?"

"Yes," she said untruthfully.

"I have sons—*arba'a,*" he told her, and held up four fingers.

"Good—*taib,*" she said, trying to sound cheerful about this empty landscape with only a dim moon to light the way, and of course it was growing cold—deserts were always cold at night—and her coat hung on a hanger in the closet of the Cham Palace in Damascus. After a bone-jarring drive of nine or ten miles she saw a scattering of lights flickering ahead, and as the truck grew closer she realized they were lanterns placed on the ground at intervals between what appeared to be tents, from the shape of them. At a distance the moonlight picked out one solitary large building, black against the night sky. Reaching the first tent—and it *was* a tent—Salim braked.

"I stop," he said and pressed his hand on the horn, the sound of it piercing the silence.

A young man stuck his head out of the tent, observed the truck and walked toward them, scowling. Caught in the headlights of the truck he was a tall young man with a

lean, very tanned face, tousled dark hair, an
unshaven jaw, his eyes hidden by glasses
that glittered in the light. He was wearing
shorts, a heavy sweater, and thick boots.

Salim stepped down from the cab and
said proudly, "Your *umm* I bring to you."

Mrs. Pollifax winced at this, but apparently the young man wasn't aware that *umm*
meant *mother,* since he only smiled and said
pleasantly, "Welcome," as he helped her out
of the truck.

"No luggage?" he asked politely.

"N-n-not with me," she stammered, shivering with cold.

"Of course," he said, and turning to Salim
he spoke to him in what sounded like fluent
Arabic, which startled Mrs. Pollifax, puzzled,
and in the end alarmed her. She could only
fumble in her purse for the money still owed
Salim and press it into his hand with an embarrassed *"Shukren,"* after which she and
the young man watched the truck drive
away in a cloud of dust. Mrs. Pollifax dared
say nothing; she only waited.

With a smile he turned to her. "I doubt
that Dr. Robinson's still awake, he's headman here at the digs. We're shutting down

soon, you know. At the end of October we pack up. Law of the land."

"I see," she said.

"And you must be tired, also cold," he added. "We'll find you a tent—you can share Amy Madison's, she's from Australia. Ceramics are her specialty. You'll have to check in tomorrow, of course, we've a few guards at the site and—"

She glanced up at him sharply.

"To guard against theft—but that can wait." He stopped and looked down at her with amusement. "Mind telling me whose *umm* you are?"

"Oh," she said, startled. "Yes . . . well, that's something the driver misunderstood."

He nodded and said casually, "Your forehead's still bleeding, the bandage looks red with blood. I think we forget Amy for the moment, I'll take you back to my tent where I've a first-aid kit and blanket."

She said nothing. There suddenly seemed no way to explain her arrival at eleven o'clock at night in Salim's pickup truck, exhausted and without luggage and with a bleeding forehead; she could only remember how desperate she'd been to get out of Tadmor and she thought drearily, *I must have assumed that I'd have a very clever explanation by now, but I'm too tired to be inventive.*

"Actually I've a second cot in my tent," he said, opening the flap of canvas for her to enter. "Vido Castrelli left two days ago, so you might as well bunk here with me. No sense in waking Amy, we retire early here because we start work early mornings, while it's cooler."

"I see," she said, and sat down on the empty cot, still shivering. "What are you excavating here?"

"An Umayyad caravansary." He was lighting a kerosene lamp; once it was lighted he brought out his first-aid kit and examined the bandage on her forehead. Frowning, he said, "It's pretty well stuck there so this will hurt."

It did hurt. "This is antibiotic ointment I'm applying," he explained. "You sure have one big and brutal gash here but I think it'll be all right. I'll put a thicker bandage over it. Had a tetanus shot lately?"

She nodded, grateful that he did not ask where, how or why she'd arrived with such a nasty gash on her head.

Bringing out a blanket he wrapped it

around her, and then handed her a tin of sardines and a fork. "Eat," he said. "In return for telling me who the hell you are and why you're here, of all places."

Two sardines and a warm blanket brought her slowly back to life. "I'm Emily Reed-Pollifax," she said, and hesitated before adding, "and I'm here to look for a man named Bazir Mamoul."

"Bazir Mamoul!" he exclaimed. "But he's a shepherd."

She nodded as she disposed of a fourth sardine.

"I remember the name," he said, frowning. "He wandered in here needing water— but it was *weeks* ago. Mustafa, one of our workers, knew him. But what makes him so—" He stopped, his eyes narrowing. ". . . so important."

He had an interesting face, but not as boyish as she'd thought at first glance, closer in age to thirty, she decided, and definitely clever and inquisitive. "He has news of interest that I'm here to inquire about," she said primly.

"Yes, but how did you hear about this Bazir Mamoul?"

"News gets around," she said vaguely. "What's *your* name?"

He studied her carefully. "My name is Joe Fleming and I insist"—he was suddenly very serious—"on knowing how you learned about us here, and about Bazir Mamoul."

She sighed. "I think it's enough that I'm here and looking for him. His arrival was . . . well, noted."

His gaze was thoughtful. "The Damascenes are great sellers of fine rugs," he said. "Have you perhaps met a boy named Abdul, possibly in the souk?"

Startled, she said, "We've met such a boy, yes."

"We? Who is 'we'?"

She sighed. "There *were* two of us, but my companion was attacked and taken away by two policemen in Tadmor, which is how . . ." She pointed to her bleeding forehead. "And he was arrested."

"Good God, and you came along—without him—after all that?" He hesitated and then, "It's just possible," he added, "that I'm the person you're looking for."

She stared at him blankly. "I'm looking for Bazir Mamoul."

He smiled. "I can assure you that I'm a

bona fide junior archaeologist but I just happen to have been asked to . . . shall we say, pass any news along that I hear out here in the desert, such as what Bazir Mamoul happened to speak of to Mustafa when he stopped here for water."

Surprised, she said, "Do you mean it was you who . . . if not for you . . . I see. . . ."

"Yes, but I think we continue this in the morning," he said firmly. "You're obviously still in shock, hurt and tired. We understand each other; that's enough. Have you finished the sardines?"

She handed him the empty tin.

"Good, I'll turn in now, we'll talk in the morning."

"One question," she said. "Something *must* be done about my friend Farrell. Is there any way to communicate from here with the embassy in Damascus and tell them he's been arrested?"

He considered this. "Barney has our shortwave radio; we order our supplies through it. Whether it's powerful enough to reach Damascus I don't know—depends on sandstorms and weather. But that will have to wait for morning." He blew out the flame in the lamp, tossed a pillow to her cot and lay down on his. "In the morning we talk," he repeated. "In the meantime, *Allah yimis-sikum bi-kheir.*"

"Meaning what?"

"Meaning 'May thy night be happy.' "

It was barely light when Mrs. Pollifax opened her eyes to find that her host of the night was sitting on his cot thoroughly shaking each of his boots. Seeing her sit up he said, "Scorpions, you know. They love shoes."

"Mine seem to be still on my feet," she said, regarding them with interest, and surprised at how suddenly she'd fallen asleep. "I must have been really tired."

"Lady, you were a mess," he told her frankly. "I don't mean that insultingly," he added. "I mean you looked on the verge of collapse, to which I happily add that you look an entirely different person this morning. Breakfast is in forty minutes, it's in the main tent." He reached for a jug of water and poured a small amount into a canvas basin. "Precious stuff in the desert, water. If you care to wash your face . . ."

She plunged both hands into the basin and splashed cold water over her face.

"What I've been wondering," he said, "is how on earth to explain you to Dr. Robinson. We're a pretty tight group here, and on a very tight budget, too."

She said quickly, "I can pay for my breakfast."

"I've decided," he said firmly, "that instead of being my *umm*"—he grinned at her—"you could be my aunt. American aunt touring Syria, stopping off briefly to see her nephew. Do you mind being an aunt?"

She laughed. "Why not? It seems to be my role just now. No scorpions?"

"Not this morning," he said, lacing up his boots. "Now do you mind telling me why you're looking for Bazir Mamoul? If I remember the story he told Mustafa that I passed along it concerned—"

"Not until you tell me who *you* are," she countered, "trusted as you must be to pass along news to certain rug merchants."

He shook his head. "Actually I've never met him, it's Abdul I meet. *Someone* has to drive to Damascus twice a month to pick up supplies we can't get in Tadmor, and it's an assignment I've asked for, so twice a month—on the same day—I lunch at the Al-Arabi restaurant where Abdul is stationed outside selling baskets or whatever, and we pretend to haggle over a sale. We've become friends, and he trusts me, but he's said only that his father sells rugs in the souk. Since just about every fourth merchant in the souk sells carpets—"

She interrupted him to say, "You're still not telling me who you *are*."

He said quietly, "*Not* CIA, if that's what you're thinking. I suspect you are, but I'm not."

"But you must have some connection—to pass along news."

"Very slight," he said, and when she looked at him skeptically, "It began when I was a graduate student—in ancient history at the university—and was paid a very small stipend for my teaching stint, I can assure you. When Dr. Robinson accepted me three summers ago—a real honor to be chosen out of so many applicants, even though there's no money in it—I couldn't afford even the plane fare to Syria. My cousin—he has a desk job at the CIA—said he thought he could scrounge up some money for airfare if I . . . ." He smiled wryly. "If I would pass along any local news: mood of the workers, droughts, diseases, rumors, all vague and sounding innocent. Anyway, I was greedy for the job and frankly thought my cousin was just being kind, but my airfares have continued to be paid for very mysteriously. You're the first indication that any of my feeble reports—mostly agricultural—have ever mattered. Does that satisfy you?"

"So you've been here for three summers, then?"

He nodded. "This is my last one, though, because I've finally landed a good, *very* good job teaching Arabic and Arab history beginning in February. Now it's your turn. What's it all about, you being here? To have come so far—damn risky, too."

"Fair exchange," she said. "It's due to a young American woman who was—" She stopped and began again. "Six weeks ago—seven by now—a plane was hijacked and landed at the airport in Damascus, and thanks to this young woman the lives of over two hundred passengers were saved. She was quite a heroine, interviewed in the airport on television, and then in plain view of the camera she got into what is believed the wrong car waiting outside, and hasn't been seen since. In a word, kidnapped. Surely you heard something of this?"

He shook his head. "My radio ran out of batteries in August and we mostly get static anyway. I seem to remember Barney saying something about a hijacking but that was weeks ago, and if that's why you're here I don't see what *you* can do."

"Find her, of course," said Mrs. Pollifax. "If she's still alive. The embassy thinks she's dead, but if Bazir Mamoul overheard an American girl talking in the desert some-where I'm here to learn where. I want to find him." She added crisply, "I'll need a guide, and a Land Rover, or a camel or whatever transportation is available out here."

He said in astonishment, "You expect to find Bazir Mamoul just like that—and by yourself? This is a *very* big desert."

"If he herds sheep," she pointed out tartly, "then he can be found where there's grazing. That's a start, isn't it?"

"You know deserts?" he said, surprised.

She smiled. "A little, yes. I've money, rather a lot of it. I can pay any guide very well who can help me find Bazir Mamoul."

"You're nuts—crazy."

"Of course," she told him cheerfully, "but what I need from you is advice, not comments on my sanity. Can you help? At least until Farrell—" She stopped, not wanting to think of what he must be enduring. *It's up to me now, up to me,* she repeated silently, bracing herself.

He was scowling at her words, looking owlish with his tousled hair, glasses and boyish face. "We have one Land Rover here," he said, "and Dr. Robinson would *never* agree to loaning it. One of the workmen—Argub—brought two of his camels with him, but . . ."

"Then I'll go on a camel," she told him. "American tourist who's lost her tour group."

His frown deepened. "Of course he *might* loan the Land Rover during one of our noon siestas, but . . ." He shook his head. "Not today, though. It would need . . . well, negotiating. And meeting you."

"Then let's go to breakfast and have me introduced," she told him. "There's also Barney with his shortwave radio; the embassy should be opening in an hour or two. You'll ask him to try to get through about Farrell? John Sebastian Farrell."

Joe said wryly, "I think I liked you better

last night before I learned all this." He grinned. "So come along, Aunt, and meet everyone and see what we're doing here."

By daylight Mrs. Pollifax had a very different view of the encampment; in the darkness she'd not seen the excavations, their many levels meticulously marked off by rods, nor the long stretch of open, canvas-shaded worktables extending out from the one adobe building that was the field office.

Joe said, "The caravan route between the Euphrates and Damascus ran through here. What we've found is either an Umayyad *khan*—inn, or caravansary—you can see two of the vaulted arches we've uncovered—or possibly a military outpost. . . . After all, the Qasr al-Hirt is only about thirty miles from here. Good morning, everyone," he said as they reached the long dining tent. "Look who's arrived last evening—my Aunt Emily Pollifax, removing herself from a guided tour to say hello. Dr. Robinson . . ."

The man at the head of the table politely rose, looking startled: tall, spare, with a short gray beard, his face shadowed by a wide-brimmed hat. He said doubtfully, "Yes er that is, welcome."

Following this, names were flung at her:

Barney from Brooklyn—she took special note of him—Fritz from Austria; Amy Madison, whose tent she'd almost shared last night; Julie and Curtis Lowell from California; Awwad, their Syrian archaeologist; and Branmin, supervisor of the workmen. At the second table sat the workers: Argub—with two camels, she remembered; Mustafa—she noted him especially, too—Fayah, Ali, Hamed, Hassan, Mahmud . . . the remainder blurred.

Room was made for her at the table next to Dr. Robinson and she at once began to artfully overwhelm him with conversation: how she wanted to learn *everything* about the Umayyads that her nephew researched, how she longed to see more of the desert, and while she waited for her cousin, delayed in Tadmor, would Dr. Robinson possibly allow her to help in the work so long as she didn't get in the way?

Across the table Joe listened to her with amusement; *The witch,* he thought, *she's certainly determined to get that Land Rover.* Her offer to help was masterful, too, since three of their party had left early: his bunkmate and Amy's, due to university commitments, and Cecil Burton for a family emergency, leaving them definitely short-handed.

With breakfast finished Dr. Robinson excused himself and Mrs. Pollifax caught Joe's eye and said, "Barney, please?"

"Ah yes, Barney," he said. "Good man, Barney, ex-wrestler, ex-army." He called him over, saying, "My aunt has a question to ask you."

She liked Barney at once, older than Joe, a friendly bear of a man with broad shoulders, a battered nose and a cheerful face, the sort of brash New Yorker with whom she was familiar, and she shook his huge hand.

He grinned. "We assumed all of Joe's relatives would be Umayyads. What can I do for you?"

"Could you get a message through to Damascus on your shortwave radio? To the embassy, for instance?"

"Damascus!" he exclaimed. "Hell no—if you'll excuse the language."

"Why?" asked Joe. "Weather?"

He shook his head. "Not enough power. What we have here is really a ham radio, its frequencies are in the middle-range band—enough to reach Tadmor—but for Damascus I'd have to have a radio with a high-frequency range—three to thirty hertz, and the government wouldn't like that. I could forward a message to Tadmor and ask it be sent to Damascus."

"Oh dear," she said, frowning. "But would the embassy know it came from Tadmor?"

He looked puzzled. "Of course."

She turned away. "I'll have to think about that, Barney, thanks."

He nodded and left, but not without a last curious glance at her.

"Why do you have to think about it?" asked Joe.

She sighed. "I was so naive last night. I thought . . . but it's impossible. If the message comes from Tadmor the embassy will know where we are. Or where *I* am. You see, we had a Tuesday morning appointment at the embassy for the ambassador to present his condolences on Amanda Pym's death, and for all I know they may have called the hotel by now and discovered our luggage is still there, but we've not been seen since Tuesday. They've no idea why we really came to Syria, you know—I'm supposed to be Amanda's aunt—as well as yours," she added with a rueful smile. "And they have *not* been told of the rumor that Amanda may still be alive." She shook her head. "They *mustn't* know where we are," she emphasized. *"Mustn't.* The police followed us to Palmyra but not here. Yet," she added grimly.

"And all I was doing was meeting Abdul twice a month at a restaurant," he said, staring at her with awe. "But your friend Farrell?"

She didn't reply. "I told Dr. Robinson I'd help," she said curtly, and walked away before she had to answer that question.

It was to be a long, frustrating and hot day for her, and she found work a blessing. She was shown a contour map of the site that looked like an abstract Picasso drawing; she learned that each new inch of earth had to be recorded, dated, and postholed. She was allowed to attend a flat screen set on legs and sift the excavated earth for any tiny objects or detritus brought up by spade or trowel. After lunch she took her turn at a long table helping Amy Madison assemble bits and pieces of ceramics like a jigsaw. She was shown the interior of the field office building, where found objects were stored and locked up each night: a veritable treasure house of ceramics whose fragments had been successfully assembled by Amy and shellacked; fragments of clay pots, writing tablets, bones; a tiny bronze statue, quite beautiful; a necklace of stones and a cache of coins.

And during the afternoon a line of donkeys made its way over the stones and pebbles, each carrying huge tin containers of water for them, and driven by two men in long gray skirts, black jackets and white turbans. "From the nearest village," Amy told her. "We boil the water, of course, and occasionally, when we tire of chickpeas and falafel, we have them butcher a sheep for us."

"They're shepherds?" said Mrs. Pollifax in surprise.

"Oh yes, the village must have at least a hundred sheep grazing in the fields around the wadi, and when the grazing thins they move, but it's a real boon for us. We have shish kebabs to celebrate."

"I could look forward to that," said Mrs. Pollifax.

But the best moment of a tiresome day was Joe cornering her before dinner to whisper, "You got it. . . ."

"Got what?"

"The Land Rover. For two hours tomorrow, noon until two o'clock. Siesta time."

"Wonderful!" She gasped. "Oh thank you, Joe. Now if you could just produce the miracle of a guide for me, too."

He grinned. "You've got one—me. It's the only way Dr. Robinson will allow you to be shown the desert in his precious Land Rover . . . and of course I'm your nephew, remember?" he said mischievously. "But don't worry, I've a good compass—a really good one—not to mention I was an Eagle Scout and went through Outward Bound and all that. Not such a bad deal, is it?"

She smiled. "I have the most fervent desire to hug you but I won't embarrass you. You're really offering *help.*"

"No," he said, "just a ride into the desert to show you what you're up against."

She said gravely, "I'll accept that. Until tomorrow noon, then."

7

She bunked that night with Amy Madison, a woman whom Joe had described as a tough old bird, but Mrs. Pollifax liked her. She was a faded blonde in her fifties, gruff voiced, carelessly dressed, a native of Australia and author of a book on the Umayyads, and she was not at all interested in small talk, which Mrs. Pollifax found restful after her tiring attempt to seduce Dr. Robinson into loaning his Land Rover, and a long day of work in the desert heat. She was even able to endure another morning, this time helping Julie Lowell make falafel, bean cake stuffed in bread and garnished with tahini sauce, but she watched the sun climb higher in a sky white with heat and waited patiently for the midday siesta.

When Joe drove the Land Rover up to

Amy's tent the workmen were lounging in the shade and smoking cigarettes, but the site was otherwise emptied. "So," he said, smiling. "Off we go!"

As she climbed in beside him he unfurled a map. "I've been studying this," he said. "It's hard to know where *not* to go. If we head directly south away from the highway and from the digs it could be tricky."

"Why?"

He said uneasily, "Because there are *said* to be a few military camps in the south. One of the rumors," he added dryly, "that I passed along, no doubt already known by your own people, if true. And we don't want to head west, there's a well-known military post at Khabajeb, about twenty miles from here."

"How do you know *that?*" she asked.

"It's a very poor country. From time to time there've been a few things stolen that we'd report. Food mostly, or tins of kerosene. Everything of value we keep locked up and guarded."

Peering at the map she asked, "What is that long name in capitals?"

"Badiet esh-Sham—Arabic for the Syrian Desert. We have only two hours," he reminded her. "What I suggest is that we drive for one hour, not south but to the south*east,* then make a turn and drive straight west, and, after scouting that, head back north to our camp. That should cover a fair number of miles and bring us back in time. Agreed?"

"Agreed," she said. "Sounds most efficient."

He started the engine and they drove out of camp past the field office and the privies, and soon there was nothing but flat and empty earth except for the shape of a mountain far away to the north and hazy from heat. Mrs. Pollifax had already learned that deserts were more often fashioned of grit and pebble, and only seldom the golden sweep of windblown sands shown in ads and in the movies, and she automatically braced herself for a rough drive.

"It's like a moonscape, isn't it," she said. "Is there the slightest possibility of finding sheep—or Bazir Mamoul—in this direction?"

"I've never been this way before but I'm afraid it's doubtful. Along the highway that brought you here, running from Tadmor to Deir Ez Zor, one sees flocks of sheep. They stop traffic when they cross the road, and we can try that direction another time—Dr. Robinson willing—but if this shepherd saw this girl you speak of, it had to have been well away from highways and villages, and his stopping at our camp for water suggests he'd been looking for his lost sheep on this side of the highway."

Mrs. Pollifax nodded.

"Who is this girl, anyway?" he asked. "Other than her name, I mean. Amanda, you said?"

"Amanda Pym. Not much known about her except that she came from a small town in Pennsylvania, both parents dead, one of them recently. We couldn't risk bringing photos of her. A rather plain young woman, twenty-three or -four, and looking—to be frank about it—rather dowdy."

There was no further conversation; the Land Rover had been stripped to essentials, and although it was topped by canvas to shade its passengers there was no windshield, and an occasional stirring of air sent dust back into their faces. They had been driving for perhaps half an hour when the earth ahead of them began to rise, the pebbles grew larger and they bumped up and down over holes and hillocks.

"Are the tires sound?" Mrs. Pollifax inquired rather anxiously, thinking it time to speak. "I mean, if a tire goes flat have you a— oh, look!" she cried, pointing to a patch of green.

They stopped and left the car to look, and, "Sheep have been here, yes," said Joe, picking up a handful of dried dung.

"But not recently," she said. "Not much grass left."

"No, they cleaned out the best of it and it hasn't rained since. By George," he said, turning to her, "I'm beginning to feel like a detective."

She smiled at him. "Welcome! Shall we go on? We've thirty minutes left before turning west."

They continued more slowly, looking for other patches of green. As they approached a more impressive rise in the ground Mrs. Pollifax said suddenly, "There's something on that hill, Joe, it looks like a sign. See it?"

"And a wire fence," he added, and driving closer he braked. Peering ahead he said, "Can't see what it says, my glasses are foggy."

"It's in Arabic, isn't it?"

They left the Land Rover to walk closer.

"Oh dear," said Mrs. Pollifax. "Not *all* in Arabic." Underneath the musical scrawls of Arabic there was a line in French and then in English that read, OFF-LIMITS. KEEP OUT.

They looked at each other with interest, and Mrs. Pollifax said, "You could wait in the Land Rover."

"Of course not," he said crossly. "Can you crawl?"

She nodded. "I can crawl, yes."

Side by side they crept to the top of the hill and peered over it. "Tents," she whispered.

"Not Bedouin," Joe said grimly. "Bedouin tents are black goat hair; those are army tents."

"Not necessarily," she whispered back. "You have the same khaki tents at your camp, but there are only four here and two long ones."

"Mercifully at a distance from us," Joe pointed out, "and not a single human being in sight. It's deserted—abandoned."

Mrs. Pollifax assessed the camp with a critical eye, noting how the hill surrounding the camp looked man-made, surely not at all natural, since it appeared to embrace the tents like a large horseshoe, making the site resemble an amphitheater. There were shrubs growing here and there, and several stunted trees, and in places the grass grew knee-high. It was hot, the sky a cloudless blue and empty, until a hawk or kite in the distance interrupted the silent and lifeless scene. "Did you happen to bring binoculars?" she asked.

"Good grief, yes," he said, "I'll go back to the car. I brought the usual gallon of water, some bread and the map and I think the binoculars are in the knapsack. I'll fetch them."

When he returned he handed them to her. "What are you looking for?"

"I thought something moved," she told him.

"Moved? In this empty place?"

"Moved," she said, lifting the binoculars to her eyes, and adjusting them she suddenly gasped.

"What?" he whispered. *"What?"*

She handed them to him. "See if you can see what I do. Four people—in camouflage seats—seated in a row, over by the tents, and staring out at this empty place and I hope not at us. They're quite distant."

Joe wiped the dust from his glasses, and

when he lifted the binoculars to his eyes he whistled faintly through his teeth. "I see them. With notebooks. They stare at the shrubs and grass and trees and—darned if they don't write things on paper. Four of them. And you're right—camouflage."

Puzzled, she said, "What does that mean?"

He said grimly, "It means we should get the hell out of here and damn fast."

"Why?"

"Because I think this must be a camp for training snipers. Ask Barney, he was in the army and knows about snipers. It means there could be someone hiding three feet away from us under that nearby shrub, for all we know. It's like a game, training snipers . . . the four with notebooks are writing down what they see, which may not be much if they're new recruits." He backed away in alarm. "What we don't want is for them to see us, too."

Mrs. Pollifax reached for his binoculars. "I want to look just once again. To where I saw something move before." One glance and she nodded and returned them. "You're right, there's the toe of a boot protruding from that second shrub. It can't be easily seen from their side when it's barely visible from here, and so much closer. It must have twitched for me to see it. And there's a bird in that stunted tree—a dead one, it has to be because it doesn't move." She suddenly felt a chill that she couldn't explain. She said, "If only you had stronger binoculars—"

"Let's *go!*" he pleaded. "For God's sake let's get out of here, Mrs. Pollifax."

"—so we could see the faces of those four people taking notes."

But there were no stronger binoculars available, and they slid down the side of the hill and walked back to the Land Rover which, far enough away as it was, still seemed suddenly too close to what they'd seen.

They had almost reached the car when Mrs. Pollifax stopped, frowning. "Look, Joe, there's been a fire over there," she told him, pointing. "The earth's black, someone's burned something there."

"So they were cold or hungry and cooked something. *Don't,*" he said flatly. "I'm not stopping for anything now until we get back to the safety of the camp. We could be shot if we're seen here, or at the very least arrested."

But Mrs. Pollifax was already on her way to the circle of blackened earth. "I'm curious," she said, "there's something dark blue sticking up out of the charcoal, something that didn't burn. You haven't a trowel, have you, or a knife?"

"No," he said bitterly. *"Or* a shovel. *Or* permission to be this near a posted, off-limits training camp."

With her fingers Mrs. Pollifax was brushing away the char, digging deeper, and with her fingers she brought up a tiny triangle of stiff, shiny blue cardboard with a scorched *T* at its edge that looked as if it had once been gold. Puzzled, she said, "This is strange."

"What's strange?"

"The feel of this, it's familiar in some sort of tactile way." She turned over the scrap to study it: the fire had run fiercely up the back of the card, blackening all but two letters and three numbers and she sat back, staring at them.

"Please—let's get *out* of here," Joe pleaded, glancing nervously over his shoulder.

She nodded and silently they returned to the Land Rover. Joe quickly started the engine, turned and headed a mile back the way they'd come before he stopped the car. "Well?" he said. "And what on earth have you been searching for in your purse?"

"My passport," she told him, drawing it out. "And look—it has the same midnight blue color and the same texture—it matches! I ought to know, I've had to show it often enough on my way here. And see the gold *T* in the top corner, forming the last of the word *Passport?*"

"You mean a passport was burned in that fire? An *American* passport?"

She nodded. "Take a look at mine closely." She held it out to him. "The back of the cover or jacket is plasticized—the fire would have loved destroying *that.* Now turn it over and see what's behind the *T* on the front of my passport."

"Okay," he agreed. "Running along the bottom of the page is 'USA Reed-Pollifax,' space, 'Emily,' and below it a long series of numbers."

"Yes, and now look at what we found in the fire. In the back of the *T.*"

"Not much," he said. "The letters YM, and below it three numbers, the rest unreadable. This means something?"

She said softly, "It could mean a great deal when you realize that Amanda's last name is Pym—spelled P-Y-M. And when you place it next to my passport it's precisely where my name appears."

"Good God," he said, "you think it could be hers, then?"

"According to the story that Bazir Mamoul told, he peered over a small hill just as we did."

"I'm in over my head," Joe admitted. "You actually think she's there, in that camp?"

"It scarcely seems possible, but she could be." She frowned. "It's interesting, their burning this outside the camp, they took great care to dispose of it at a distance from the fences. They were careless about it," she said, pointing to the remnant she'd uncovered. "There could be more there if only we—"

"You scare me, Mrs. Pollifax, you really scare me."

She smiled. "I know. You've been ever so kind just to do this."

"Never mind that, the question is what she'd be doing there, and why."

"Yes," she said, "but the larger question is whether she's still alive."

He glanced at her sharply. "She was alive seven weeks ago, at least *someone* American was alive, according to Bazir Mamoul."

"But for what purpose?" she murmured, frowning. "And why? And how do we— There must be stronger binoculars at your camp."

Startled, he said, "You can't go back, it's too dangerous."

"I have to remind you," she pointed out gently, "that I'm here to find and bring her back to America if she can be found."

"But alone? By yourself?"

"Farrell will find me," she said with more confidence than she felt. "The police will learn he's American, and surely the embassy will hear of it. We were met at the airport by a Mr. Jacoby from the embassy, so they know we're here, and we had that appointment with them that we didn't keep. They'll make an official protest at once."

"You hope," he said dryly. "And if he's freed, how do you know he'll ever find you?"

"Because I know him." *And he knows me,* she thought. "We were both on our way to this camp when he was attacked and arrested—he knows the directions—so where else would he look for me?"

Joe laughed a little shakily. "And none of this worries you?"

"Not," she said, "when we've just found what looks to be a remnant of an American passport that could be Amanda Pym's buried in the middle of the Syrian desert."

He said curiously, "You've told me *who* she is, but what was she like, this Amanda Pym?" With a glance at his watch he started up the engine and they began their return to the camp.

"On television," said Mrs. Pollifax, "she was—as Farrell said—the most unlikely heroine he'd ever seen. Mousy. No personality. A little frightened but perhaps she was only shy. She said yes and she said no and the interviewer was thoroughly frustrated trying to pry some words out of her."

She saw that Joe was frowning. "You'd think she would *flaunt* what she'd done, be pleased, excited. It's odd . . . and she'd saved the lives of how many people?"

"Over two hundred."

"That's a lot of people, how on earth did she do that?"

"There were two hijackers. The plane had been on the tarmac for several hours when suddenly she left her seat and walked up to the nearest hijacker and asked for his gun."

"You're kidding! Just like that?" He shook his head. "Weird! I've always had my head in books; I've not much curiosity about people—unless they were Umayyads," he said wryly, "but now I find myself curious about your Miss Pym, too."

Good, thought Mrs. Pollifax ruthlessly, *the more curious the better if it earns another trip in the Land Rover.*

If not, she decided, one of Argub's camels . . . because of course she had to go back.

Tell Khamseh was still noon-quiet when they drove in, the sides of each tent open for any stirring of air that might rise. At this hour, with the sun overhead and lean of shadows, the khaki tents merged with the khaki-colored earth, the only dark note the deep grids of the excavation.

Across the compound Amy Madison left the tent she was sharing with Mrs. Pollifax and strode toward them. She said, "Your name *is* Pollifax?"

Mrs. Pollifax nodded.

She said curtly, "The most disreputable man arrived an hour ago, he said he knows you. I put him in my tent; he's been hurt." She said sternly, "I don't think Dr. Robinson is going to like all this coming and going, it's very disturbing."

"A man? Hurt?" echoed Mrs. Pollifax, and jumped out of the Land Rover to race into Amy's tent.

He was lying on the cot that she'd occupied during the night, one arm in a sling, dark bruises under one closed eye, unshaven, a cut on his left cheek and his clothes in tatters. *"Farrell!"* she gasped.

He opened one eye and said weakly, "Duchess?"

Amy and Joe had followed her into the stifling tent. Amy said, "He just . . . walked in, asking for you. His wrists were in terrible shape. You *know* this man?"

"I certainly do," said Mrs. Pollifax. "He traveled to Syria with me. Farrell—my God, the police did this to you?"

He shook his head. *"Not* police."

"Not police?" she said, puzzled.

Farrell struggled to sit up and then sank back with a groan. *"Not* police," he gasped.

"Whoever they were they know all about us and why we're here, and they were going to kill me. Duchess, somebody very definitely doesn't want us to find Amanda Pym."

8

Mrs. Pollifax spent the next hour seated beside Farrell in Amy's tent and bathing his
face in precious water, raiding Joe's first-aid
kit for antibiotic ointments and applying
these to his bleeding wrists. She was able
to reassure herself that his arm was only
bruised from shoulder to wrist, but not broken. He was sleeping deeply, from time to
time waking up to say blankly, "It's *you?*"
and then, "Thank God," and fall asleep
again.

In late afternoon Joe stuck his head in
the tent and said, "How is he? I brought you
food."

"I don't think he can eat yet."

"I brought it for *you,*" he told her, and
looking down at the sleeping Farrell said,

"So this is your Farrell. My cousin, I suppose?"

She laughed. "Yes, unless you'd prefer a brother."

"Well, *eat.* It's last night's falafel, quite safe. The only generator we have in camp—a small one—runs on diesel and is strictly for the refrigerator and our food. Can he be moved yet, do you think? Amy seems a bit unsettled about having a man in her tent."

Farrell opened his eyes. "I'm not deaf. Of course I can walk."

He did not precisely walk, but limping and leaning on them both he was conveyed to Joe's tent, where Mrs. Pollifax propped him up and Joe said, "He's all yours now, it's back to work for me," leaving Mrs. Pollifax and Farrell to look at each other with interest.

She said quietly, "What happened, Farrell?"

"Knocked me around a bit," he said wearily. "Threatened. Information was demanded: who sent me, who did I work for, who told me Amanda Pym was alive. Then they tied me to a post for the night—standing—and said they'd kill me in the morning if I didn't talk. That sort of thing." His eyes moved to her bandaged temple. "I don't know how you made it here, Duchess, but I'm sure glad to see you." He managed a wry smile. "Damn good luck they didn't haul you away, too, but I gather they think women here have no value."

"I should be insulted," she told him lightly, "but for the moment I'm relieved. How on earth did you get here in your condition?"

"From Tadmor? Walked. Stumbled. Kept away from roads. Hid in a pickup truck last night that brought me three hours nearer. Walked the rest of the way. Am I developing a black eye?"

"Afraid so," she said, and very casually asked how he got away from his captors, and from Tadmor.

"Sheer luck," he said grimly. "That post I was tied to—one rope around my middle, both hands tied behind my back—had a nail sticking out of it, probably a hundred years old but sharp enough. One of the men slept, and the one guarding me grew careless—or bored."

"You mean—"

He nodded. "For hours I worked on the rope around my wrists—that one blessed nail. They didn't seem to notice. Nearly dawn when I freed my hands. They'd not found the knife—the one I bought in Damascus, in the souk, remember?—and with my hands freed I sliced away the rope that tied me to the post. Jumped out of a window and ran—some godforsaken street at edge of town." He hesitated, frowning. "But there's something else, Duchess."

"What?"

"I never saw their faces but one of them—I swear that he mixed German words into his English and Arabic. *'Guten Gott!'* he said once, and then, *'Ich haben'* before he gave a start and returned to Arabic. And once the word *'achtung,'* which even I know means 'attention'."

"German!" she exclaimed.

He nodded. "A small detail, but interesting."

"Bewildering!"

"Unfortunately," he said, "and I'm sorry as hell about this, but I'm not going to be of much help to you for at least another day."

Joe, opening the tent flap, walked in saying eagerly, "I heard that. Have you told him yet what you and I discovered today?"

She liked the "you and I," especially when

spoken with a touch of pride. It was just possible . . . With a pointed glance at Farrell she said quickly, "This is Joe Fleming—I'm *his* aunt now, too—and he's proved ever so resourceful and helpful today, and we did discover something I think *very* important." She added demurely, with a glance at Joe, "He might even consent to offer *more* help until you're on your feet again."

Farrell grinned. "Roped him in, did you?" He gave Joe a critical glance and appeared to like what he saw. "So what *did* you find this morning?"

Joe winced. "Wish I could stay but she'll have to tell you. I took that minute from work to move you here to my tent, but I've got to go back, or Dr. Robinson—well, you know."

He rushed out, and Mrs. Pollifax sat down and proceeded to tell Farrell what they'd found on their hard-won trip in the Land Rover, and when she had finished she brought out her passport, and from her pocket the remnant they'd rescued from the ashes of a fire.

Examining them both Farrell looked up and said, "Congratulations, Duchess, what you found is very definitely a scrap of a passport, and an American passport, and one cannot ignore that YM. Have you any idea how far away that mysterious camp is from here?"

She nodded. "On our way back I kept an eye on the Land Rover's odometer. I've not done the arithmetic yet but it was about twenty-two miles, and map-wise our direction was somewhat diagonally south-southeast from here."

"Think you can find it again?"

"I want to," she said cautiously. "I want to see what else was burned in that fire."

He nodded. "According to our friend in Damascus in the souk—Omar—the camp's privy was very near to where you did your spying. Probably a pit in the ground. Did you notice it?"

She shook her head. "I didn't look for it, I was in a state of astonishment, and Joe was frankly scared. We certainly didn't linger."

He thought about this. "The fire sounds the most important of all—to confirm she was there or still is. It's what the State Department—not to mention Carstairs—will want to know. But damn risky, Duchess—don't forget what Bazir Mamoul said about their privy being very near to where you

must have done your spying . . . anyone using it just might look over that hill and
see . . ." He looked down at his bandaged
wrists and swore. "Damn it, Duchess, it's
going to be another day before I can help.
Wait for me—don't go alone, it's too dangerous."

She said nothing. Farrell obviously wasn't
thinking clearly yet because they couldn't
afford to wait for him; only forty or more
hours ago he'd escaped from two men in
Tadmor who would be looking for him now,
and who would no doubt widen their search
beyond Tadmor very soon. They couldn't *afford* time, it was necessary to act with haste.
To be found here would be disastrous, for
Dr. Robinson and his work, and for Farrell
and herself, as well as for any hope of finding Amanda Pym. She only said gently, "Do
lie back, Farrell, and concentrate on getting
well. And don't *worry.*" She left him to find
Joe and ask about a camel.

"You're crazy," Joe told her, climbing up
the ladder out of Site Two. "A camel? And
at night?"

She said tartly, "I can scarcely go by daylight, can I? We were lucky this morning, but another time we might be seen, and I want to do some serious digging. There was something about that fire . . . as if they'd just dumped things there, lit a few sticks and left. If the flames didn't consume all of that passport then it's possible the fire died away before anything buried deeper could be reached. There could be *more* to find."

He said grudgingly, "Well, it's true there's not much kindling in the desert, just dried dung and bits of twigs. But you can't go on a camel, it would take hours. They're *slow.*"

"Then I'll walk," she said stubbornly.

He looked at her with amusement. "Blackmail, *Khaleh* Emily?"

"*Khaleh?*"

"Arabic for 'aunt.' "

"To be called a blackmailer shocks me to the core," she told him.

"I'll bet," he said, grinning. "I suggest we borrow the Land Rover—okay, steal it once it's dark—drive it within a few miles of the place, and walk."

"We?"

"So I'm curious," he admitted. "There'll be a moon tonight, not full for two more days, but enough to find the way there without being conspicuous." He added wryly, "Dr. Robinson likes you, and of course I impressed him by returning his Land Rover so punctually. He's very stern about such matters. I can tell him you'd love seeing the desert in the moonlight."

"What time?"

"Whether he says yes or no, about seven, once work stops?"

"I'll be ready," she told him. "What *do* they all think about Farrell limping into camp, bloody but unbowed?"

"I told them he fell."

"Fell?"

"Off a wall."

"And do they believe that?" she said incredulously.

"I doubt it," he said, grinning, "but Dr. Robinson does. His head is where mine usually was—back among the Umayyads. Very scholarly chap." His face clouded. "We've got to be careful; we all had to be cleared by the government here—had to be—and I don't want Dr. Robinson to get into any trouble. I think tomorrow I'd better approach him about pitching a tent for you and Farrell outside the camp. A bit of dissociating, if you get what I mean: aunt and cousin guests for a few days, until my cousin recovers and all that?"

She smiled at him. "I do like you, Joe."

He grinned. "The mischief I never got into, growing up, seems to be taking over at the ripe age of twenty-seven."

"No mischief?"

He shook his head. "Both my parents were history professors, I never got around to rebelling, it would only have bewildered them. How can you rebel against parents who live in another century? My rebellion was taking up with the Umayyads."

"The Umayyad," she said. "When did *they* live?"

He said promptly, "They occupied the country in A.D. 661, made Damascus their capital, and were overthrown by the Abbasids in A.D. 750."

"I see . . . and you were an only child?"

He nodded. "See you at seven, I've got Dr. Robinson to approach at dinner. The usual menu, of course."

"Not for me," she said, and went back into the tent to worry about Farrell, and to watch him carefully. Congratulating him on his escape was meaningless, she knew. She had once, in Hong Kong, undergone torture—she still carried the scars on her back—and she remembered very well the state of her mind when she'd been rescued; mercifully it had been temporary, but she knew that what Farrell needed now was the commonplace, a familiar face, work to do, and sleep to heal a mind still dazed by meeting with the worst that one human being could inflict on another.

He greeted her cheerfully, however, and knowing how resilient he was she was hopeful. "There's food and water on the table beside your cot," she told him. "I'll be going out for an hour or two this evening. Since I'm posing as Joe's aunt—and a mere tourist—it appears to be obligatory that I see the desert in the moonlight."

If he suspected more, he did not say so. "Then tell Joe to be quiet when he gets back because I plan to sleep and sleep and sleep." He grinned. "Only way I can be of use to you by tomorrow. Sleep always does it for me."

Whatever Joe said to Dr. Robinson proved successful. The Land Rover drove up to her tent at seven o'clock, and climbing in beside Joe she found herself sitting on a mound of cloth. "What's this?" she asked.

"Djellabas," he said. "Borrowed from Mustafa and Argub. As a joke, I told them. They're in case we're glimpsed from a distance."

"Joe," she said, "I'm discovering new depths in you by the hour."

He laughed, and they set off in the direction they'd taken that morning, headlights shining until—with a glance at his compass—he announced, "Here's where we start walking."

The moon was high in the sky, shedding a soft and hazy light that outshone the stars. The air was cool and refreshing, so cool that Mrs. Pollifax was glad to pull on the old brown djellaba woven of wool. *Borrowed car, borrowed djellaba, and borrowed spoons for digging,* she thought, and found it quite pleasant, walking in the night. "I wonder if we'll see any lights at that camp," she murmured.

Joe shook his head. "Doubtful. No electricity. They could have a generator but it's more likely they've kerosene lamps, as we do, and those earthworks are too high to see *them.*"

She had left her purse back in Amy's tent, but Joe had borrowed a small burlap sack from the storeroom. When at last they sighted the hill in the distance they began the job of looking for the darker circle of charred earth. For this the moonlight was of little help and they lost a precious twenty minutes before Mrs. Pollifax stumbled across it, and at once she sank to her knees, spoon in hand. She dug while Joe kept watch, and without heed to what she uncovered she dug deep, spading everything—sand, pebbles, debris—into the sack that Joe held open for her. Extending the search beyond the fire she left a sizable hole behind her into which Joe made a hurried attempt to kick pebbles and earth.

When at last she said, "Enough!" Joe slung the bag over his shoulder. "This must be how grave robbers feel," he said as they walked away, not slowing their pace until the hill melted into the horizon, no longer visible.

When they returned to Camp Five it was nearing eleven o'clock and the site was dark except for the soft glow of lanterns set among the tents. A guard was asleep on a bench outside the field office, and roused at the sound of the Land Rover. Joe called out a few words in Arabic and he lay down again, satisfied.

"What we need is a hand screen," Joe said. "To sift the wheat from the chaff. Tired?"

"No," she lied. The cut on her temple had come to life and was throbbing, and she was beginning to realize that she had arrived at the camp roughly forty-eight hours ago and that she, like Farrell, had endured a difficult trip. With her normal energy depleted she was drawing heavily now on reserves. *Or adrenaline, bless it,* she thought, but was not about to admit it. "I'm fine," she told him. "I could never sleep without knowing if we found *something.* Where's that hand screen?"

Joe found one left on the ground near Site Two. They carried the sack and the screen to a nearby lantern and sat down beside it. "We do this sort of thing every day—tirelessly," said Joe, dropping handfuls of dirt and pebbles across its surface.

"Paper!" cried Mrs. Pollifax suddenly. "Look, scraps of white paper!"

"I'm looking," Joe said. "What do I do with them?"

She unwound her white headscarf and he

gathered together the scraps of paper and dropped them into it. When they had emptied the burlap sack they had culled a neat pile of scorched and torn pieces of paper. "Except, alas, no passport," she mourned.

Joe reached for a crumpled sample from the collection and whistled faintly through his teeth. "No passport but there's an American here *somewhere.* Look at this!"

He handed her one of the scorched remnants and by the light of the lantern she saw English print, something torn from a book, and leaning closer she read, *Poems by Emi*— and below it, *I Was Hun*— Fire had eaten away the rest, leaving its ragged edge brown with singe.

For a moment, tired and sleepless, Mrs. Pollifax thought she was going to cry. "English," she whispered.

Joe, plucking out another scrap said, "Hey—there's more English and this one's written by hand; it says 'taught to be incons . . .' " He looked at the quantity of scorched papers and shook his head. "This is going to be like gluing together shards of Ommayan pottery!" One glance at Mrs. Pollifax's face in the light of the lantern and he forgot their contraband. "Good God," he said with a gasp, "you've lost your bandage and it's starting to bleed again. You must be exhausted, we should never, never have— You need sleep."

"I—I think you're right," she said with a wry smile.

He helped her to her feet, gripped her arm and escorted her to Amy's tent. "I'll take these scraps with me—I'm rather good at jigsaw puzzles—and see what sense I can make of them. I'll do it with a flashlight outside my tent so I won't wake Farrell." He added crossly, "You should have told me; I should have— Oh damn it, sleep. All *day* if you want, *Khaleh* Emily."

"Thank you," she told him gravely, walked into the dark tent, glanced at a sleeping Amy, found a blanket and without bothering to remove her clothes lay down and at once fell asleep.

9

In Langley, Virginia it was ten o'clock in the morning when Bishop picked up the telephone to hear that Amman, Jordan was calling: that would be Rawlings, of course, in their Jordan office. "Hold on a minute," he told him. "I believe he's on another line."

He buzzed Carstairs and then walked into his office to see whether he was ordering lunch sent up from the cafeteria, or was still talking with Jacob Mboro in the Sudan. There had lately been a number of calls to and from the Sudan and Bishop, curious, and knowing little about the country, had looked it up in their library. Carstairs had been more helpful. "Largest country in Africa," he said. "Underpopulated and needy. To simplify, draw a line roughly across the middle, at Khartoum: the top half is Arab, and mostly Muslim; the bottom half of the country are the natives, Christians or animists, and they want autonomy. Call it civil war or guerilla war; it's been going on for years."

He opened the door in time to hear Carstairs say, "Good, I'll see what I can do," and cut the connection. Seeing Bishop he said cynically, "I must be getting old. Life was so much simpler when half the world backed the Soviet Union, and the other half lived in terror of the Soviet Union. Remove the Cold War and internal conflicts multiply in countries by the week."

Bishop said meekly, "Rawlings is on line one from Jordan, sir."

"Ah yes, Rawlings," he said, and to Bishop, "I'll want this recorded, turn on the machine, will you?" Turning to line one he said, "Carstairs here."

Bishop sat down and waited for further instructions.

Rawlings, young and still fairly new to the Middle East, said, "Yes, sir. I want you to know this call's being scrambled."

"That bad?" said Carstairs lightly.

"Well, it's from Damascus, sir, it just came in. The usual way."

"Yes?" Carstairs's voice was no longer flippant but deadly serious. "Talk."

"From A-511, sir, code name Omar. The following message to be forwarded to you. It begins, and I quote, 'Carpets not selling well, two sent to Palmyra.' " He hesitated, and then continued, " 'Fareeq killed at Palmyra—have confirmed, reconfirmed, and verified assassin unknown to police. Assassin mingled with group of tourists and escaped.' That's it, sir, end of agent's message."

Showing no immediate expression, Carstairs said noncommittally, "Thanks, Rawlings, I'll keep in touch." He hung up and exploded with a "Damn and damnation!"

Bishop, frowning, said, "Fareeq? I don't recall an agent named Fareeq."

"Not under that name, no—you'll find him in our top *top* classified secret file." Carstairs added savagely, "He was one of our most trusted surviving informants over there, and a damn fine man—and he's dead? He was never a man to be careless . . . the question is why, and by whom."

Bishop said doubtfully, "Can you really *believe* he wasn't killed by the police?"

"If A-511 says not by the police then it was not by the police. Omar has connections, he's reliable. Which means, who killed Fareeq and why, and what the hell was he doing in Palmyra?"

He reached over and switched on the machine and listened again to Rawlings's message from a world away. "Two rugs sent to Palmyra," he murmured, and then, "Oh God."

"What?"

"It has to mean he's made contact with Mrs. Pollifax and Farrell and he sent the two of them to Palmyra, presumably to meet Fareeq."

"And now he's dead. . . . Was he under surveillance, do you suppose?"

Carstairs shook his head and said drearily, "So far as I know, Fareeq has never been under suspicion, and he'd be too clever to be followed and not know it. It's more likely that it's Pollifax and Farrell who were being followed, which is fairly normal procedure over there, and Farrell and Pollifax knew this."

"Then how—"

"I don't know," said Carstairs grimly. "My reaction, quite frankly, is one of horror, it implies that others may have been following the two of them. Palmyra's a major tourist site, it's possible their police surveillants lost sight of them, or assumed they'd be staying there an hour or two, and took a break. Whatever happened—if that was the case— the fact that Farrell and Pollifax stopped to speak to Fareeq signed his death warrant."

"But that means—" Bishop stopped.

"Exactly," said Carstairs, tight-lipped. "Get me the Cham Palace in Damascus, Bishop, and after that the embassy."

The next thirty minutes were busy ones for Bishop. The hotel reported that Mrs. Pollifax and Farrell had ordered a car for Palmyra on Tuesday; so far as they knew they had not returned yet, since their keys remained untouched at the front desk. Calling the embassy, Carstairs was told with a hint of aggrievement that an appointment with Amanda Pym's aunt had been made for Tuesday morning and that neither she nor her companion had appeared.

"I'm sure they're all right," Bishop said with all the brightness he could muster, even as he felt anxiety blossoming and taking root.

"Really?" growled Carstairs. "My conclusion is that news of two people arriving in Syria to inquire about Amanda Pym has been leaked. Widely shared, one might say, with people who know a great deal more about Amanda Pym than we do, and if they also know that she has no aunt it means they know Amanda *very* well."

Bishop dropped his pretense of optimistic cheerfulness. "Then they'd still be following Mrs. Pollifax and Farrell, these people who aren't the police?"

Carstairs glanced away, his jaw tightening. "Possibly. Or after murdering Fareeq—" He stopped, and with a steadier voice said, "Or after killing Fareeq there's the possibility that Mrs. Pollifax and Farrell would be next on their list."

Oh God, thought Bishop, *here we go again.*

"It suggests very strongly," said Carstairs grimly, "that Amanda Pym is still alive. It also makes her very, *very* important to someone over there, and the question is *why* is this girl so important to them?"

"If Miss Pym is still alive . . ." began Bishop.

"At this moment," growled Carstairs, "I'm far more interested in whether Emily Pollifax and Farrell are still alive, damn it. Call Rawlings back, and instruct him to keep his line open for Omar night and day, and report to us any further news at once."

10

When she opened her eyes the next morning Mrs. Pollifax saw that Amy had gone and that Farrell was standing over her with a cup of steaming brew. "You slept late, Duchess, I've brought you coffee. Very *strong* coffee, I might add. And young Joe has been telling me how you arrived here, and at what hour and in what condition."

"I was luckier than you," she said lightly.

The tent was stifling and she glanced at her watch and was startled to see that it was nine o'clock. "I did sleep late," she admitted, and sitting up she gratefully accepted the coffee and after two sips made a face. *"Very* strong—enough to clear the sinuses!" and with a glance at Farrell's face, "Aside from your black eye, which is turning purple now, how are *you* feeling?"

"Much restored," he told her. "Now tell me about this Joe who's adopted you."

She laughed. "It's a long story," she told him, "but he's a real archaeologist. He just happens to have a cousin in the CIA who subsidized his getting here three years ago when he was broke—*if* he'd pass along any news of interest in this part of the country. It's he who reported the story Bazir Mamoul told one of the men here when he stopped for water. He's not a pro; he's never met Omar, but twice a month he goes into Damascus to pick up supplies and chats with Abdul."

"I'll forgive him for snoring then," Farrell said. "It sounds like the two of you have been busy as hell, Duchess."

"I don't think hell is connected with busyness," she said thoughtfully. "Hell is more like boredom, or not having enough to do, and too much time to contemplate one's deficiencies."

"Which I was doing all yesterday," he said. "What on earth possessed you to go back into the desert last night? And what did you find? Do you realize Joe was up practically the entire night laying out pieces of paper and studying them? He refused to explain, too."

"I'm surprised that he didn't. We went back to dig more where the passport was found. In the dark. Hoping to find more— and we did, Farrell. Those scraps of paper we brought back seem to be torn out of a journal handwritten in *English.*"

He thought about this, frowning. "Not quite enough to satisfy the State Department, Duchess. Not enough for them to demand action. We'd have to actually *see* Amanda Pym, wouldn't we? To be certain she's there, and still alive?"

"Oh yes," she agreed, and was silent, considering this. "The only hope of actually seeing her would appear to be at the privy— everyone there would visit it—although it's terribly rude to spy on people at such a time."

"Why?" asked Farrell. "We're not planning to sell photos of them to a tabloid." He frowned. "Can you draw me a sketch of the camp as you and Joe saw it on your daylight trip?" Seeing that a lined notebook lay on the table next to Amy's cot he ripped off a sheet and brought it to her, along with a pencil. "Draw it."

Obligingly Mrs. Pollifax put down her cup of coffee and drew an elongated circle. "The tents were down at this end," she said. "Far enough away so that we needed binoculars to see the people there. I remember a tree here . . . and here . . . and here," she continued, sketching in trees ". . . and high grass here and here, and the tents. . . ." She drew four small triangles and two large ones at the far end.

"And the privy must be near where you spied on them, it has to be." He reached for her pencil and added a square with a question mark.

"So what do you think?" she asked.

He smiled. "I think, Duchess, that I've quite recovered—a trifle wobbly, but my brain is operative, thank you—and I think it's time for me to make *my* contribution, and we can't afford to stay at this camp much longer."

He was thinking, of course, of the two sadistic men who would be looking for him. "And your contribution, if one may ask?"

"Once it's dark tonight, I'll establish myself at the base of the hill and lie there until I hear some activity, then crawl to the top and give a quick look, just as Bazir Mamoul did. The moon's almost full tonight, I should be able to see *faces.*"

"And they could see yours," she pointed out tartly.

"I suppose you're right," he admitted. "Duchess, at the beginning of this you said we'd need imagination, ingenuity and resourcefulness . . . think of something!"

"I said that?" She sighed, and considering this for a long moment suddenly brightened. "Birnam Wood!"

"Birnam what?"

"*Macbeth,* remember? 'He'll not be vanquished until Birnam Wood moves to Dunsinane' . . . camouflage! Dig up one of those stunted woody shrubs, and as soon as we get there—it'll be dark—plant it at the top of the hill so that its leaves and twigs form a screen. They won't notice a *bush.* We can take turns creeping up the hill—but it'll be cold—and look without their seeing us."

"*Macbeth,*" he mused. "Unfortunately my vaudeville parents never played *Macbeth.* Flamenco dancing was their gig, but the idea has potential. Let's do it."

At this point Joe interrupted them by walking into Amy's tent and announcing that it was almost lunchtime. "And Amy will be wanting her tent for a nap after that. What are you planning?"

Mrs. Pollifax told him what they were plotting to do and he looked alarmed. "But you'll need the Land Rover again, what on earth can I tell Dr. Robinson this time?"

She said ruthlessly, "Tell him that *Farrell* wants to see the desert in the moonlight. How is your jigsaw puzzle of scraps coming along?"

He said with a wry smile, "It's rather like archaeology—when one translates what someone long ago wrote and felt—except this is someone contemporary, and maybe still alive. What she's written, I mean." He added eagerly, "We had one semester on Babylonia at university and there was an ancient Babylonian prayer that I memorized that really explains . . . well, how exciting archaeology can be, hearing a voice from thousands of years ago. Care to hear it?"

Farrell shrugged and said indulgently, "Sure, why not?"

"Good . . . it's a prayer, you know." Closing his eyes he was quiet for a moment and then he slowly recited, " 'I am silent and in tears and none takes me by the hand. My God, who knowest the unknown, be merciful . . . in the midst of the stormy waters come to my help, take me by the hand. . . .' "

They were moved to silence until Mrs. Pollifax said softly, "How beautiful—and how eloquent."

Farrell said gruffly, "When would that have been written?"

"Long before Christ was born. I've often wondered—"

Mrs. Pollifax nodded. "Yes. Who and what and if."

"And that's the way it sort of is *now,* trying to piece together these scraps of paper that could turn out to be torn from a journal Amanda Pym kept."

"What have you found so far?" she asked.

His eyes dropped. "Not much yet," he said vaguely. "So *many* scraps."

Mrs. Pollifax gave him a curious glance but said nothing.

"I'll work on them some more this evening, after you've gone," he said quickly. "And of course I'll ask Dr. Robinson about the Land Rover." He hurried out of the tent, and Mrs. Pollifax found it surprising and a little amusing that after his intense interest in accompanying her on the previous evening he appeared indifferent about their return to the sniper camp tonight. The scholar in him had surfaced, and he appeared now to have become involved in deciphering, not a Babylonian prayer, but an Amanda Pym.

Joe had succeeded in securing the Land Rover for them, taking to Dr. Robinson a substantial payment for the gas they'd used. If this was blackmail, thought Mrs. Pollifax, it was at least for a worthy cause, and they set out, she and Farrell, as soon as the sun had vanished in a burst of orange, scarlet and gold.

Once the Land Rover had been left behind, the three-mile hike seemed longer to Mrs. Pollifax than it had been the night before, and the moon was alarmingly bright. "I think," she decided, "that we should begin the Birnam Wood scheme a bit early. The moon seems awfully bright. If anyone should be looking, if they have a watchman or a guard . . ."

"Say no more," said Farrell.

Joe had borrowed djellabas for them again, and each of them wore one—Mrs. Pollifax's was too long and she frequently tripped over it—but even two wandering no-mads could be suspect. After a brief recon-naissance they found two small thorny shrubs, four feet high and bearing enough fleshy green leaves to hide behind. After la-boriously digging them out of the earth they advanced, carrying them like flags and feel-ing very foolish. Once in sight of the hill they set the bushes down in front of them to make sure they'd not been seen; after an interval they moved closer, pausing from time to time until they at last reached the base of the hill.

"Nobody shot us," said Farrell with some relief. "I'll go first, I've not seen the camp, you know, and I'd like to get a good look at it." Binoculars in hand, and shoving the tree ahead of him Farrell crawled to the top. Mrs. Pollifax watched him dig a hole with his bare hands, and once he had securely planted the shrub she saw him huddle down behind it and train the binoculars on the camp. When he returned he said, "A few lights in the long tent, one in a small tent. And I could spot the privy, it's not far. A deep pit, and fortunately they've not filled it in yet, or moved it, which they no doubt do from time to time."

"Good," she said, pleased. "And now we wait."

It was not long before they heard voices, and as they grew louder Farrell clawed his way to the hilltop to peer through his screen of dried leaves. With a shake of his head he returned. "Three men," he whispered. "Kicked a few pebbles into the pit and left."

A shivering Mrs. Pollifax said, "I'm stiff with cold, let me have a turn next."

He handed her the binoculars and she struggled up the hill to press her body against the earth that still contained warmth from the sun, and for this she was grateful. She studied the moonlit compound and the dark outlines of the tents. After a fifteen-minute wait she saw two figures leave one of the small tents and head in her direction toward the privy. She lifted the binoculars to her eyes, and observing their walk and slimness she thought, *Not men this time.* They came nearer, unzipping their camouflage suits as they walked, and when they reached the privy below, and some twelve feet away from her, Mrs. Pollifax was able to look from one face to the other—one dark, almost swarthy, with thick eyebrows, and the other—*"Yes!"* she whispered exultantly: the same face, deeply tanned and thinner now, same nose, same large eyes . . . *Amanda Pym.* She had found Amanda Pym—she was alive and she was here.

She remained very still, her eyes straining to see into which tent the two girls disappeared: second from the right, she decided, unless the moonlight deceived her. Only then did she slide cautiously down the hill to Farrell. "I saw her," she whispered. "I *saw* her."

"I didn't hear any voices," he protested.

"They didn't speak, but it was Amanda. Two girls, one of them Arab, one of them Amanda."

"So she's still alive," he said in amazement. "And here of all places. Hell, that does it, Duchess, let's get back to the Land Rover and to the flashlight. I borrowed Joe's compass—we'll want to take our bearings very carefully so we can report exactly where she can be found."

"Where she can be—" She stopped. He meant a report to the State Department, and she gave him a quick glance but said nothing, suddenly realizing that Farrell's wounds might be quickly healing on the outside, but that he was carrying them with him inside, buried deep. Farrell was afraid.

As I ought to be, too, she thought, wondering how on earth they'd ever get back to Damascus, but she was remembering Amanda Pym's face in the moonlight, thinner now, cheekbones sharpened into gauntness, looking younger in her camouflage suit than she'd appeared on film in that ill-fitting thrift-shop suit. It was apparent that for Farrell this was enough, but Farrell was refusing to remember what Carstairs had said: he had very clearly stated that he wanted Amanda Pym back if she could be found.

And now they had found her.

When they returned to the camp there was still a light in the tent that Joe shared with Farrell. They found him seated on his cot, leaning over a small tray table covered with sheets of paper, a jar of paste and the jigsaw scraps from the fire collected into a bowl. He glanced up, glad to see them. "Any luck?" he asked, and his eyeglasses glittered in the light from the kerosene lamp.

"We found her," Mrs. Pollifax told him eagerly. "She's there, I *saw* her."

"Wow," said Joe. "But that's great—wonderful—congratulations!"

"We found her," Farrell said, nodding, "so I think we can leave here in the morning."

Mrs. Pollifax said sharply, "Farrell—"

"Leave? You can't leave," Joe said angrily. "You can't leave now."

"Of course we can leave," Farrell told him stiffly. "We found her. I've taken the compass bearings of where the camp is, they can find it on their satellites—"

Mrs. Pollifax said coldly, "Yes and what, send paratroopers down for her? In *Syria?*" To Joe she said in a quiet aside, "He had a rough time when he was captured, he's thinking of those men who must be looking for him now."

"Of course they'll be looking for him," Joe said indignantly. "They don't want you to find Amanda Pym, and now you've outwitted them and found her, and you're just going to *go?*"

"Farrell," she said gently, "you're tired."

"I'm not tired," he snapped. "Obviously you think we should try to get her out of that camp but you must realize it's impos-

sible. My God, it's a sniper camp; they don't
just learn camouflage and how to hide—
they have guns and know how to use them.
We've found her, that ought to be enough.
We owe her nothing."

If Farrell startled Mrs. Pollifax by turning
into a stranger, Joe startled her even more
by saying, "You owe her a *life,* damn you. I
know a lot about her, and you can't just
leave her there, it's too cruel."

Abruptly Mrs. Pollifax sat down on the
opposite cot. "You've pieced together
scraps from her journal, haven't you. What
is it you know about her? There were certain
doubts in the department. . . ."

"I didn't tell you before, I hadn't finished—
still haven't," he said, "but to hear you say
you found her and are going to leave her
there is more than I can stomach."

"Why?" demanded Farrell.

"It's only guessing on my part but I think
I know now why she was so reckless to dis-
arm that hijacker at the risk of her life."

"Then tell us," said Mrs. Pollifax.

He looked at her doubtfully. "I'd rather
show you . . . show you *both,*" he added
with an angry glance at Farrell.

"Oh for heaven's sake," Farrell said crossly.

"You can look for yourselves at what I pieced together," he told them. "There's still a pile but I went through them piece by piece until I found matches."

"To what?"

"Look for yourselves. I've lined them up chronologically, because after a lawyer was mentioned her mother wasn't, so I think her mother died recently. But decide for yourself."

Both she and a reluctant Farrell took their places at the table and looked at what he'd pieced together.

Mother furious about . . .

. . . more hand-me-down clothes from . . .

. . . explained why no money for college, I can't . . .

Mother said the meat cost . . .

Mother insisted I . . .

Mother said I couldn't . . .

. . . to poorhouse, she always brings up poorh . . .

. . . tired, so tired. Of scrimping, scrimping, scrimping and . . .

. . . she died at 3 A.M., and . . .

. . . a safe-deposit box tomorrow, the lawyer so kind and . . .

They lied, lied, lied, LIED!!!! All these years!

. . . what do I do with . . . it all?

. . . a fool, wearing new . . . clothes, where would I . . . wear them?

More stocks sold, another check to-day . . . $83,000, I wanted to tear . . . it up, it's so meaningless.

. . . was taught to be incons . . . picuous, I end up invisible.

Invisible, thought Mrs. Pollifax, jarred by the word. *She seems to have moved through life not being noticed at all,* Carstairs had said. And if Amanda Pym had been invisible in Roseville, Pennsylvania, what would have been her experience in Egypt, shabby and timid, traveling alone?

Farrell said dryly, "A lot of mothers there."

"Certainly a demanding one, perhaps an invalid," suggested Mrs. Pollifax.

"I'd say a tyrant," said Joe fiercely. "There are others that I can't match up yet, a lot about her longings to go to college but—"

"Couldn't afford it," put in Mrs. Pollifax, nodding.

"Yes. The last one I patched up are lines torn from an Emily Dickinson poem called 'I Was Hungry.' "

"It's not one I'm familiar with," said Mrs. Pollifax.

"Care to hear the lines of what's left of it?"

"Another Babylonian prayer?" asked Farrell cynically.

Joe paid him no attention. "There are lines missing, but they're in print, not copied. She must have torn it from a book to carry in her journal." Picking up the third sheet of paper, he read:

I had been hungry all the years;
My noon had come to dine;
I, trembling, drew the table near,
And touched the curious wine.

'Twas this on tables I had seen,
When, turning, hungry, lone,
I looked in windows for the wealth
I could not hope to own.

"The rest of that is scorched but there are two other lines," Joe said.

> I did not know the ample bread,
> 'Twas too unlike . . .

"The only remaining line not scorched was," said Joe, " 'The plenty hurt me, 'twas so new, Myself felt ill and odd.' " A thoughtful silence followed these words.

"So what's your conclusion?" asked Farrell reluctantly.

Joe said angrily, "I think her parents lived like misers; I think she had a very depressed and depressing life. I think what made her a 'heroine' at the hijacking was suddenly realizing that she didn't know how to live—nobody had ever shown her how—and suddenly she didn't care. She may even have hoped they'd kill her."

Shocked, Farrell said, "You mean . . . suicide?"

"People do reach that point in life," pointed out Mrs. Pollifax softly. "When there's no hope. It happens." *As it did to me once,* she remembered.

Farrell's glance had fallen to his bandaged wrists and Mrs. Pollifax guessed that he was looking, not at his wrists, but at his fear of being captured and in pain again, probing and examining his fears, and admitting to them at last. With a twisted smile he said, "All right, you've made your point, Joe. We can't leave her, but how the hell we get her out of here is beyond me."

Joe said eagerly, "I'd help. The camp closes in ten days; I could quit early."

"To do what?" growled Farrell, and turning to Mrs. Pollifax, he added, "Well, Duchess? Imagination, inventiveness, resourcefulness, remember? Just how do you think two people—"

"No, *three*," put in Joe.

"—could invade a camp of snipers, find Amanda Pym, and get her, and all of us, out alive."

"I'd have to think," she said calmly.

"Then *think*, damn it."

Mrs. Pollifax began thinking. Her thoughts had a tendency to move in a straight line, and with a simplicity that often startled other people. It would be folly, of course, to attempt to storm a camp full of snipers when they had no weapons, and she did not bother to consider this: one had to work with the tools available. She crisply divided the problem into three: how to get into the camp, how to snatch Amanda Pym and get out, and how to get away without being followed. It would have to be at night, of course. In her mind's eye she pictured the camp, its length, its breadth and the height of the wire fence, and she nodded.

Joe said eagerly, "You've thought of something?"

"Yes," she said. "Sheep."

11

"Sheep?" said Joe blankly.

"Sheep?" repeated Farrell. "You said *sheep?"*

She nodded. "Sheep," and turning to Joe, "You have to think carefully before you offer help, Joe, this would *not* be risk-free, it's not a matter of researching the Umayyads or the Babylonians, or digging up bones and pottery."

"I know," he said, nodding. "This is real. It feels time I get involved in something real. I could be useful, couldn't I?"

"Very useful," she said, "since you speak Arabic and we don't. Do you know if anyone in the camp has wire cutters?"

"Barney brings a tool kit with him every summer; we always kid him about being Mr. Fix-It. He *must* have wire cutters."

Farrell, listening to this, said again, "But sheep, Duchess? What on earth—"

"It's quite simple," she told him. "If a fair-sized hole can be cut in their fence, what could be more overwhelming and confusing than a herd of sheep moving into and through the sniper camp? Baaing all the way, I hope," she added. "And in the dark."

Farrell shook his head. "What you're thinking of is a stampede, Duchess, but it's cattle that stampede. *Not* sheep."

She said coldly, "They'll stampede if pushed. Joe, Amy told me the village people who bring water every few days raise sheep. She said at least a hundred, did she exaggerate?"

"No, not at all," said Joe eagerly. "A hundred at least. What they raise here are fat-tailed sheep, because they store fat in their tails and rump. They raise them for milk and for their wool."

"So there you are," she told Farrell triumphantly, and with a glance at her watch, "You said the village is about fifteen miles away?"

"Roughly yes," Joe said.

"Sheep move slowly," she added regretfully, "and if they stop to graze it would take most of tomorrow for them to arrive, so we'll have to get to work right away."

"No rest for the weary?" murmured Farrell.

"Sleep can be snatched, but we must have wire cutters. Joe, see if Barney's awake, and if he isn't, wake him up and ask if he has wire cutters. After that it's vital the two of you get to the village, even if you have to walk—and *now,* tonight, to get the sheep moving by dawn. We can't take any chances, they've got to be here by sunset tomorrow. Where's our money?" She reached for her purse and drew out a wad of Syrian bills. Handing them to Joe she said, "Would this be enough?"

"For what?"

"To rent a suitable number of sheep for two days. You speak Arabic, thank God. Tell them their sheep will be returned to them— or most of them, one must assume. Hire one or two of their boys, too, they can help you herd the sheep and return them. But the sheep must be started no later than tomorrow at dawn."

Joe laughed. "This is crazy, really crazy. I'll wake up Barney now."

At once he was gone, leaving Mrs. Pollifax and Farrell to observe each other with interest. "Well, Farrell?" she said.

"I give up," he said, and grinned. "All I can say is, I wish your Garden Club could see you now, Duchess, sitting in a canvas tent in the middle of the Syrian desert, wearing somebody's djellaba, or whatever it's called, and plotting an attack on a sniper's camp with a herd of sheep. Incidentally," he added, "they can shoot at sheep as well as people."

Mrs. Pollifax said calmly, "I have always found that most people, awakened from a sound sleep at night, tend to lack their usual reflexes, at least for a few minutes. Besides which, the sheep will be well inside their compound before they're heard at the far end of it where the tents are." She hesitated and then, "Farrell, how are you *really?*"

"Better, Duchess." He smiled. "You lost me for a little while, you know."

She nodded. "I realize that, but I've been there, too, Farrell. . . . I didn't lose you for long," she reminded him. "And it was *very* understandable." But this was not a wise subject and she quickly changed it by saying lightly, "You may not even have to walk all those miles to the village tonight. The way

Joe is embracing the criminal life he may very well steal the Land Rover."

"Very bad influence," agreed Farrell gravely.

They heard the crunch of gravel outside and Joe reappeared, waving a competent-looking tool. "Got it," he said. "Barney was actually insulted that I thought his toolbox wouldn't include this. But we'll need more robes, won't we? The sort peasants wear— *abayas,* not djellabas. For me at least."

They had become "we," which amused Farrell. "Yes, but you might inquire about a Land Rover again for tonight."

"Oh, it's already revved up," Joe said. "I didn't ask this time; Dr. Robinson's asleep by now—"

Mrs. Pollifax and Farrell exchanged smiles at this.

"—and anyway, you paid him enough money for an entire week of gasoline. Farrell and I can sleep in the Land Rover at the village until sunup, you know, so we'll be dead sure to get the sheep moving by daylight."

"But the villagers will surely be asleep by now."

Joe dismissed this with, "Oh yes, but I

know which house the headman lives in—
the oddest houses, shaped like beehives. I
suppose it keeps them cool. Barney and I
rode back on the cart once just to see the
village, and the headman gave us tea. That's
when we saw the sheep; they'll be taking
them to the hills soon for the winter. They'll
like this money," he said frankly. "They're
really quite poor. With all this"—he brought
the wad of bills from his pocket—"I don't
think he'll mind being waked up."

"We've created a monster," said Farrell.

Mrs. Pollifax laughed. "Yes, but such a
nice one, and delightfully efficient." She
glanced at her watch. "Nearly half-past
ten—you'd better head for the village now,
hadn't you?"

Joe handed her the wire cutters. "Guard
these with your life, will you? And have a
good sleep."

Mrs. Pollifax followed them out of the tent
and watched them climb into the Land
Rover and take off, heading west this time.
Before finding her way into Amy's tent and
her own cot she lingered a few minutes in
the chill desert night, watching the red tail-
light of the Land Rover, its front lights briefly
illuminating shrubs and rocks and casting

strange shadows before it disappeared from sight, while overhead the full moon had begun its journey across a dark indigo blue night sky. Mrs. Pollifax shivered; it was terribly important not to think of what lay ahead of them, or how they would ever get out of Syria, with or without Amanda Pym. Sleep was also important, and with a sigh she entered Amy's tent to begin the long night and even longer day ahead of them.

Mrs. Pollifax slept uneasily, woke, slept, and woke again at the first hint of silvery predawn light. The night was over at last, and having slept in her clothes she wrapped herself in the djellaba, and carrying a blanket tiptoed out of the tent. The camp looked oddly forlorn until she saw the Land Rover parked in its usual place in the shade of the field office, and in surprise she hurried to Joe's tent.

Farrell was there, sound asleep and clutching an odd bundle of black woolen cloth, but at her entrance he at once opened his eyes. "Hi, Duchess," he said and sat up, rubbing his eyes.

She had to smile, for he looked a complete ruffian now, still unshaven since Damascus and wearing a four days' stubble of beard. "Sit down," he said, gesturing to Joe's empty cot. "There's much to talk about."

"Where's Joe?"

"With the sheep, on his way back by now with two boys named Rachid and Hisham. Once they started he sent me ahead, and I'll take over with the sheep when they get here and herd them toward the sniper camp. We've done a lot of talking, Duchess; after all, he's been here for three seasons and knows a hell of a lot more than we do, as well as knowing the language. I thought naively that we could cross the desert to Damascus." He shook his head. "Unfortunately Joe says it's nearly two hundred and fifty miles, so it has to be by bus."

"Ouch," she said with a shiver. "Dangerous."

He nodded. "It could be, but Joe says they don't stop the buses very often now for ID checks. One of the Deir Ez Zor buses stops at Tadmor and then goes on to Damascus—a long trip—six hours; another goes up to Homs, but he'll know which one we need. He suggests we get the bus at a village or town named As Sikhneh tonight and—"

"I know the place," she told him. "The man who brought me here was delivering food there."

"Good. He says it's the best and least conspicuous place to catch the bus, especially in the middle of the night. He's also bought some things to wear. You and I must go as Bedouins—the Pym girl, too, if we can get her out. He'll go in his American clothes because he's been on the bus before, they know him, he has all the papers connecting him to Tell Khamseh in case there *should* be a police check, and he thinks they won't bother *us—if,*" he added dryly, "we look authentic Bedouin."

"Oh dear," said Mrs. Pollifax.

Farrell grinned. "Don't worry, you just have to wear this rather dirty *abaya* and look strong and plump, and I've kohl to outline eyes—for *her,*" he added, as if to name her would bring them bad luck. "Also a black robe and headscarf for her, and cheap sandals." He shook his head. "I think Carstairs must have been psychic to have given us so much money."

"And in Syrian pound notes, too," she reminded him. "One wonders how they reach Langley, Virginia, and let's hope they're not forged! I think he knew," she added thoughtfully. "He's never given us so much before . . . he can really be uncanny at times." She frowned. "But the bus at As Sikhneh? How on earth do we get to As Sikhneh?"

Farrell hesitated. "You're not going to like this, Duchess, I didn't at first. Joe's had a little talk with Barney—"

"Oh *no.*" Mrs. Pollifax gasped. "To involve *him?*"

"Hush, it's all right. Barney said he very definitely doesn't want to know what the hell Joe's up to, no questions asked. He's a good friend, he'll ask for the Land Rover tonight to go off alone into the desert to look for another hamster."

"For a *what?*"

Farrell grinned. "It seems the golden hamster was discovered here in Syria. It's a desert creature, and Barney's tamed one and keeps him in a cage in his tent, and calls him Jack. Hamsters are nocturnal, so night is the time to look for them, and he's done it before. They're actually called the Syrian hamster, and he'll probably tell you all about them on the way. Stop laughing, Duchess."

"I can't help it," she said. "Hamsters and sheep!"

"Well, to proceed: Barney will have the Land Rover parked without lights near enough to the sniper camp for a quick get-away tonight, after which he drives us the forty or so miles to As Sikhneh and we wait there—and no doubt wait and *wait* for a bus, with Joe—traveling American—giving no indication that he knows us. From the village he's bringing loaves of *khobz*—we subsist on bread—and we can't be seen drinking bottled water, that's for tourists."

"A small sacrifice," she told him. "Farrell . . ."

"Hmmm?"

"Never mind," she said, and wished that she'd slept better. For a few days here at the digs she'd felt safe, it had been a welcome haven, but to think of leaving it now brought a sense of dismay. There was something about night, too; night was for sleep, it arrived at day's end, when one was presumably tired and vulnerable. She'd felt this way before, she recognized it and knew that it had to be tamed. There was work to do, it was why she was here.

"What is it?" asked Farrell, concerned.

She forcibly turned her thoughts away from the night to apply herself to the practical. "I think for the next hour, if someone has a needle and thread, I'll sew pockets into each of these *abayas,*" she told him. "After all, we can't dress as Bedouins and carry purses or knapsacks." And since the camp was stirring now she left and went back to Amy's tent to ask if she had a sewing kit.

It was another long day of waiting. While some of the workers continued in Site Two, sweeping and digging, measuring levels and recording them, others—Amy among them—had begun packing crates for their departure, the crates to be shipped to the Antiquities Department in Damascus, where they would be assessed, cleaned and dated, and the discoveries divided between Syria's museums and the American university that had sponsored the expedition.

Mrs. Pollifax, having sewn pockets in each robe for their passports and money, helped as much as she was allowed. Having time now to more properly observe the work still being done, she could see how the caravansary had begun to take on a recognizable shape as more paving stones of its floor had been uncovered. In Jordan Mrs. Pollifax had seen a restored caravansary, bare and stark, and bearing no hint of the travelers who in ancient times drove their camels into it, to bed down with them for the night before continuing their journey; it had seemed just another museum, and she'd not given serious thought to the romance of caravans arriving from distant and improbable places, crossing deserts and over mountain passes. Here, now, was a real caravansary emerging out of the earth, and she wondered what they'd brought so far to trade and sell.

"Bars of silver," Amy told her when she asked. "Gold and spices and silks—but most of all frankincense, which they offered to their gods. And also," she added bluntly, "they used both frankincense and myrrh as perfumes, because they didn't bathe often."

"Frankincense and myrrh!" exclaimed Mrs. Pollifax. "How biblical."

"Oh, but long before Christ was born,"

said Amy flatly. "Assyrian inscriptions have been found that refer to Tadmor as long ago as 1150 B.C., meaning that Tadmor was already on the transdesert route."

"So long ago! What *was* the route?" asked Mrs. Pollifax.

"It usually began in South Yemen—the Hadhramaut—winding its way up through Saudi Arabia, past Mecca, and from there traveled to what's now Jordan, but at Petra the caravans would split and go in different directions." She added with a sudden smile, "We've had some excitement this season, something more than shards of pottery and tablets and seals and water jugs."

"Excitement?"

Amy nodded. "I'll show you. They're not crated yet, they're in the field office under lock and key. We're hoping this could bring us more funding next year."

"Suspense mounts," said Mrs. Pollifax as they walked toward the building. "What is it?"

"You'll see. . . . You may have noticed that in Site Two we've reached the floor of the caravansary with its paving stones. One of those stones was loose, and a week ago a workman pried it up and found a cache of valuables hidden there, very, *very* old, which suggests the caravansary was here even before the Qasr al-Hirt."

"That *is* exciting," agreed Mrs. Pollifax.

"We think, from what we found, that a long time ago this inn must have been attacked by marauders, and one of the merchants—for every six camels carrying frankincense and silks he was allowed one camel for personal belongings—we think this man, whoever he was, hid what mattered most to him so the marauders wouldn't rob him of it. Buried treasure—in a great hurry—out of desperation." She admitted with a smile, "We make up stories about that man, and what might have taken place here—all of us—because what he'd buried he never retrieved. And we wonder and speculate what happened to him during the attack, whether he was captured or killed."

She led Mrs. Pollifax to a corner of the field office and removed the padlock from a separate small crate and opened it. "Just look," she said, and placed in Mrs. Pollifax's hand a necklace of medallions, each circle carved with a time-blurred face of a woman.

"Lovely," breathed Mrs. Pollifax. "Brass?"

"No, gold, pure gold . . . it just needs cleaning. In Damascus it'll be dated, but Dr. Robinson is sure that it's over a thousand years old. And here's a necklace of bone and ivory, and this might interest you," she added, presenting Mrs. Pollifax with a small pouch of amber-colored powder. "It's raw frankincense, and still fragrant. Smell it."

"Ummmm," murmured Mrs. Pollifax, sniffing, but what moved her even more was a small box that Amy handed her, in which lay a faded bouquet. "Flowers from the frankincense tree," said Amy, and leaning over it Mrs. Pollifax marveled at its being preserved in the earth almost intact: its yellow petals had faded somewhat, but each bore a heart of red in its center, and a very faint scent lingered. "And what story have you given this?"

"That's the romance of it all," Amy admitted, her weather-beaten face softening. "We like to think the bouquet was given to him by someone he loved very much. As a token, a talisman, to take with him."

"But he never returned," said Mrs. Pollifax sadly. Like Joe's Babylonian prayer, here was another ghost from the past, leaving them to wonder who and what and if, never to be answered.

"Apparently not," said Amy, placing the box tenderly back in the crate and locking it, and then, *"What* in heaven's name is that noise outside?"

Listening, Mrs. Pollifax smiled. "It sounds like sheep," and she left Amy to hurry outside.

What she saw was Joe leading a herd of sheep that stretched back almost a quarter of a mile behind him; he had kept them at a distance, on the outskirts of the camp, but they were protesting noisily as they passed: sheep of all colors—black, brown, white, cream—prodded in the rear by Joe's Bedouin companions keeping them on the move with their sticks.

Amy, joining her, said with a frown, "I wondered what had happened to Joe today." She shook her head. "Has he gone out of his mind? Such a conscientious young man, but how childish of him to play at being a shepherd!"

"There's a child in all of us," murmured Mrs. Pollifax, and was delighted to see Farrell emerge from his tent, wire cutters in hand, to relieve Joe and drive the sheep the rest of the way. Once it was dark he would begin cutting the fence, she knew, and she glanced at her watch: half-past four, a trifle late, but they should reach the sniper camp by eight o'clock, when the sun would have set. There must, she thought, be at least seventy sheep, but in any case there were far too many to count.

Joe strode toward them, grinning. "What do you think of that, Aunt Emily?" he said breezily, and to Amy, "You're looking grim, what's up?"

"You did no work today."

"I know, but since we're nearly finished here I've cleared it with Dr. Robinson that I leave early to show my aunt around the country a bit. She's not seen Aleppo; or Maamoula, where they still speak the ancient Aramic language and their blue houses march up the mountain; or Safiti—hot and humid, but I love that place—and she's only in Syria for eight more days. Right, Aunt Em?" he said with a wicked grin.

Really, thought Mrs. Pollifax crossly, *for an Umayyad scholar this young man is shedding inhibitions by the hour, and enjoying it all far too much, totally unaware that we may all end up arrested and in prison and— Oh, dear, I mustn't think of that,* she told herself firmly, must *not.*

"Got to see Barney," Joe said, and went off to find his friend, no doubt to confirm that Barney had secured the Land Rover for a hamster hunt once it was dark.

Dinner was falafel again. Argub's camels brayed; after-dinner conversation blossomed and then flagged; the sun set in a blaze of color; the lanterns were lighted, and one by one the inhabitants of Camp Five repaired to their tents. Mrs. Pollifax slipped her passport and money into the pockets of the coarse brown *abaya* she'd soon be wearing, gathered up djellabas, headscarves, sandals and Farrell's kaffiyeh, and waited.

Presently the silence was interrupted by the sound of the Land Rover. It stopped outside of Joe's tent and from his tent Mrs. Pollifax emerged, a mere shadow in the darkness. She tossed her bundle into the rear seat, climbed in beside it, and with Barney driving and Joe beside him they headed east.

12

As they sped along in the night a cloud had perversely blotted out the waning moon, and the stars shed little light. It was rough ground but Mrs. Pollifax managed to struggle into the new clothes, pulling on black baggy pants, the brown *abaya,* the white headscarf, and to exchange her walking shoes for old sandals.

"Stop here," Joe said, reaching the drop-off point. "Straight ahead two miles is the sniper camp, I clocked it."

"Right," said Barney, and handed him his flashlight. "Once the sheep are inside the camp I'll pull ahead without lights. And for God's sake—mine, too," he added lightly, "be careful."

"Barney, I love you," Joe told him flippantly. "All set, Aunt Pollifax?"

"All set," she assured him, and they began their cold walk in the dark, so dark that when suddenly Farrell rose up in front of them they were startled.

"But where are the sheep?" whispered Mrs. Pollifax.

"Behind a small rise in the ground over there." He pointed. "Hisham and Rachid are keeping them there; they were tired enough to be quiet, mercifully. And," he added proudly, "I managed to cut a really decent hole in the fence, at least five feet wide. The last lights have gone out at the camp, they should be asleep by now."

"We hope," murmured Mrs. Pollifax. "Remember, the tent I saw Amanda enter is the second one from the end. On the right."

Farrell nodded. "Yes, and you head for it just as the sheep come in. *Lead* them," he emphasized. "If you find Amanda your being a woman will be less threatening to her, but I'll be close behind, backing you up."

"And I'll follow," said Joe, "ready to hit anybody who interferes, and I've got a mean right."

Having announced this, he and Farrell withdrew to begin moving the sheep, while Mrs. Pollifax sat down at the base of the hill in the darkness to wait, hoping no scorpions were keeping her company. To quiet her nerves she tried to think of Cyrus, but she found this difficult since he was living in a world of bright lights, hot water, automobiles and books, completely foreign to her at this moment when she had become a pseudo-Bedouin crouched in one corner of a sniper's camp. What she was feeling now was akin to stage fright, a familiar mix of exhilaration, dread and suspense. *It's going to be all right, it's going to be all right,* she repeated to herself like a mantra, over and over, and was relieved when the sound of complaining sheep cut short the suspense: they were being driven toward her, and it was obvious from their protests that they did not like it at all.

She stood up, ready to escort them through the opened fence into the compound, and a moment later found half a dozen bleating sheep surrounding and nudging her. Climbing quickly to the top of the hill she slipped through the fence to receive them. Driven from behind, and having nowhere else to go they followed, trampling each other as they were pushed up and through the hole, and seeing the herd mass-

ing behind them she was stricken with remorse: it was like inserting them through the
eye of a needle but there was no time for
remorse. The camp was still dark and silent,
and with a sizable number of sheep inside
the camp Joe and Farrell were suddenly beside her, prodding the sheep forward with
their crooks, and with the herd moving faster
Mrs. Pollifax moved with them toward the
tents.

Behind her she heard Farrell say, "Faster,
faster!" which seemed quite unnecessary,
she thought, since the sheep in the rear
were being pushed hard against the sheep
in the front—and suddenly there was panic,
so abrupt that Mrs. Pollifax was almost
knocked to the ground, and—"They *do*
stampede!" she said in a gasp as they
surged frantically past her. Barely managing
to remain upright she struggled through and
over them to one side, the right side, shout-
ing, "Amanda? Amanda Pym!" and when
she reached the tent next to the end she
shouted her name again.

The flap of the second tent on the right
had been raised and a dim figure stood
there, motionless. A woman's voice from inside shouted angrily at her in Arabic, and

Mrs. Pollifax, pressing closer, looked into the face of Amanda Pym. "Come!" she shouted, seizing her by the arm.

From somewhere a man's voice shouted, "Trouble! *Jib ed-dar!* Bring the lights! And a *bundukiyeh*—my gun, fool!"

The girl seemed unaware, her eyes fastened on the sheep milling around in a panic at finding no exit. Farrell reached her side, picked up Amanda and slung her over his shoulder and, "Let's *go!*" he shouted over the noise of fifty or more outraged and bleating sheep, and Mrs. Pollifax followed, zigzagging around and over the herd and back toward the privy and the fence. From behind them a shot was fired . . . they reached the gap in the fence . . . a push and a shove . . . behind them were shouts now in Arabic, and glancing back she saw flashlights blossoming like fireflies in the compound, and then she slid down the hill behind Farrell.

Barney had backed the Land Rover to the base of the hill; Farrell shoved Amanda Pym into the backseat, Mrs. Pollifax joined her, and Farrell squeezed in beside her as Joe leaped into the front seat. Both Hisham and Rachid made a flying exit from the camp to cling to the sides of the jeep, and they took off at a high speed without lights, racing across the untilled rocky ground at sixty or seventy miles an hour. *But after all,* thought Mrs. Pollifax, *what could they possibly run into?*

After several miles of rough travel Barney stopped the Land Rover. Joe spoke in Arabic to Hisham and Rachid, and they jumped off to return to their own people, with Joe calling after them, *"Allah yisellimak!"* To the others he said, "I told them that when they start rounding up the sheep tomorrow they'd jolly well better not go near the camp, because there is *no* way to explain that hole in the fence."

"No way," agreed Farrell.

Barney turned on the headlights, and in the sudden dim illumination he turned his head to see who occupied the rear. He said, "You've certainly got an interesting passenger, is that a boy or a girl? And in a camouflage suit, no less."

In the dim light they all looked at Amanda, Farrell and Joe for the first time. It was no wonder that Barney had mistaken her sex because she'd been given a boy's haircut. The shorn hair accentuated her wide gray eyes, the line of her cheekbones, and her boyish, sunburned face. She looked, thought Mrs. Pollifax, like an urchin, and an urchin who had made herself very small in the corner, eyes wide with terror. She whispered, "Does it begin now? So soon?"

"No," said Mrs. Pollifax sharply, and to Barney, "Do drive on, this is no time to talk. Where are we?"

"Sorry. We're not far from the Deir-ez-Zor highway that runs through As Sikhneh and then to Tadmor. I'll stop before we get to As Sikhneh, since I assume this pile of djellabas I'm sitting on has some purpose."

"You bet," Joe said. "You're also sitting on my good tweed jacket, damn it, and don't wrinkle it."

Presently Amanda's head dropped against Mrs. Pollifax's shoulder and she slept. The highway was asphalt, and straight and smooth—a welcome relief—but not without traffic. A truck passed loaded with bales of cotton. "Cotton!" exclaimed Mrs. Pollifax.

"Oh yes," Joe told her. "They raise a lot of it up here." A truck piled high with melons passed, a military jeep, and an oil truck, and presently a yellow cloud of light brightened the sky ahead, and Barney drew off the road and stopped. "That's As Sikhneh up ahead. If you have things to do," he said, "this is the time."

Mrs. Pollifax turned to Amanda. "Wake up now, Amanda," she said, but there was no response. "She doesn't wake up," she told them.

Barney knelt in the front seat and turned the flashlight on her face. "She could be drugged. I'm not asking why but she may have been into sleeping pills."

"Or given them," said Joe.

Farrell leaned across Mrs. Pollifax and slapped the girl, first on the left cheek, then on the right cheek, and she opened her eyes, startled. "We're getting out of the car," he told her.

Obediently Amanda climbed out, but as Mrs. Pollifax began unzipping her camouflage suit she asked despairingly, "But oh where are you taking me *now?*"

Joe, staring at her, looked visibly shocked. "We're Americans, Amanda, we're taking you back to America—*Inshallah,*" he added under his breath.

"You know me?" she faltered.

"You're Amanda Pym, and we're going to change you into an Arab now, wrap your head in a scarf and put sandals on your feet, and *all* of our lives depend on your being a very proper young Arab woman, very very quiet, so we can get you out of this country."

"Americans," she repeated dazedly.

"In spite of two of us looking Bedouin we're all Americans," Mrs. Pollifax told her crisply, "and we're going to have to take a bus soon to Damascus. I'm to be your mother, and Farrell here will be your father. This is Joe, by the way, but he will not speak to us after we get to the bus, do you understand?"

Amanda's eyes were fixed on Joe's very American tweed jacket and this, thought Mrs. Pollifax, somewhat reassured the girl. Gently leading her away from the others she unzipped her camouflage suit, peeled it away and off, and held out the dark *abaya. Dear God, how thin she is,* she thought. "Trust us, Amanda," she told her. "Put this on." When she had finished robing her and winding a black scarf around her head and exchanging her boots—good ones, she noted—for cheap native sandals, she rearranged her own headscarf. Signalling to Joe he joined them, and in the glow of the flashlight he darkened Mrs. Pollifax's eyebrows and thickened them, and then, "Hold still," he told Amanda, and carefully outlined her eyes in kohl. Moving to Farrell he, too, became almost unrecognizable with his stubble of beard and thickened brows. During this redesigning of them Mrs. Pollifax noticed that Barney kept at a distance, his back turned to them. He had told Joe he wanted no knowledge of what he was up to and she found this amusing, considering the enormous help that he'd given them; by now he must have a very good idea, and still he asked no questions. Joe, she thought, had a very good friend.

Amanda was led back to the Land Rover, and they climbed in beside her and drove the last few miles to As Sikhneh without comment. It looked to Mrs. Pollifax like a sleepy truck stop in the Midwest at this hour, with a few neon lights, a blue and yellow gas station with signs exclusively in Arabic, and the town behind it in shadow. Barney slowed the Land Rover; there were already mysterious shapes of people beyond the lights, huddled together and apparently sharing food while they waited for the bus. The lights also illuminated a scattering of broken plastic jugs and empty soda cans across the ground, and an orange wall plastered with advertisements for Mandarin soda, Lucky Strike cigarettes, and one primitive drawing of a smiling Hafiz al-Assad.

Barney reached into the back and gave to Mrs. Pollifax a small burlap bag of—

"What?" she asked.

"Grapes, and a few dates for protein," he told her. "And here are your tickets, I made reservations for you yesterday on the bus." He hesitated, and before she could thank him he said with a mocking smile, "Delighted to have met you, Joe's aunt." With a smile, a salute and "Cheers!" he turned the Land Rover around and left them . . . left them in the semidarkness in what felt to Mrs. Pollifax the middle of nowhere.

"We sit," she said in a low voice.

Joe nodded. "But don't speak again," he whispered, and to Amanda, "Talk later, you're an Arab now, you understand?"

She stared at him without expression but nodded. She appeared a shade more alert now and gave Mrs. Pollifax a curious, sidelong glance, as if seeing her for the first time; Mrs. Pollifax thought she even saw an attempt at a smile that quickly vanished. They had come a long way for this young woman; there were so many questions she wanted to ask of her that it was frustrating to realize they must travel like mutes.

Pointing to the orange brick wall Mrs. Pollifax led Amanda to it and they sat down on the ground, their backs against it, and after a minute Farrell joined them. In the dim light he looked alarmingly tired—haggard, really—and while this added an interesting dimension to his disguise it worried her. She, too, was tired, and the cut on her forehead, quiescent all day, had begun to ache again—but *she* had not been tied up and beaten, or walked for miles. She thought of how Farrell must have reached deep inside of himself for the strength to carry on so cheerfully—as he so often had done in the past—and she reached for his hand. Leaning close she said in a low voice, "Sleep, Farrell, you need it—I'll wake you."

He gave her a wry smile and nodded. She released his hand and he closed his eyes, but whether he slept or not she couldn't know, but it had become her turn now to remain alert and on guard. To keep her eyes from closing she occupied herself by remembering the bizarre circumstances under which she and Farrell had met: as two strangers tied up back-to-back in a remote airport in Mexico, later followed by a torturous escape out of Albania. . . . How many incredible people—a whole collage of them—she'd met on her trips for Carstairs, she thought, and her memory went back in time to a man who had been very dear to her, and whose real name she would never know, a man who had said, "If only you had been born Bulgarian, *Amerikanski,* we could have changed the world!"—as perhaps, in a very small way, each of them had. And remembering Tsanko she felt a rush of gratitude for the strange detour her life had taken that had so enriched and changed her . . .

. . . And had brought her now to this moment of waiting in a desert town of Syria, where she could only count the people who must be looking for them: the two mysterious men searching for Farrell, and surely by now a few outraged members of Amanda's sniper camp, and she wondered for how long the three of them must remain exposed and vulnerable here until the bus came to take them . . . but where? The rug man in the Damascus souk was their only hope. If they could find him again.

13

Barney had deposited them at As Sikhneh at close to midnight; it was three o'clock in the morning before a gaily painted bus came into sight, and by that time they had been joined by four more people, all men, and Mrs. Pollifax made a point of observing them closely. Three arrived together and, without any interest in Mrs. Pollifax, Farrell, and Amanda, continued a lively conversation with much laughter; she gained the impression they were workmen on their way to a job. The fourth man walked out of the darkness alone, not far from them, and gave each one of them an interested glance as he passed to take his place in the shadows. Because of that glance, casual but thorough, Mrs. Pollifax felt a small sense of alarm and took note of his appearance, so briefly seen: a long face and nose, thin mustache, dark skin and piercing eyes, a man wearing a simple gray djellaba, a checkered kaffiyeh, and brown sandals. She decided it would be wise to watch him.

As the bus came to a stop Joe, rising from his perch on an oil drum, yawned, stretched, stood up and murmured, as if to himself, "The Damascus bus at last—hooray!" and they lined up to enter. Farrell, awake and alert now, secured the long seat in the back for them, and although Mrs. Pollifax was able to observe each passenger as they climbed into the bus she did not see the man with the piercing eyes; he was not among them. *Surprising,* she thought; he had simply vanished.

The bus drew away with the three of them huddled side by side in the rear, a shabby peasant family with Mrs. Pollifax clutching the small sack of food on her lap, and if Amanda looked frightened it was hoped that it would be mistaken for the shyness of a young unmarried Arab girl. Farrell immediately fell asleep, or feigned it, and as the bus began its drive to Tadmor Mrs. Pollifax, deprived of reading material and conversation, stared out of the window and watched

the sun rise, and with it the sudden appearance of houses and fields and people that
had been wrapped in darkness earlier: they
passed a girl astride a donkey with metal
water containers hung on either side of her
saddle, like panniers; there was a glimpse
of low black Bedouin tents in a distant field,
and of sheep scattered over the hillsides.
Pickup trucks loaded with cargo passed
them, as well as oil trucks and small Mazda
and Sukuki passenger cars.

She wanted to say, "Oh look!" She
wanted to question this young stranger sitting beside her, wanted to ask her so many
questions: what she'd been training to do
in that sniper camp; why her life had been
spared; what she'd endured; who the people were with whom she'd spent almost two
months—but she mustn't. She wanted to
talk to Farrell, not to ask, "What next?" but
simply to talk: to *communicate.* She had
worn disguises before, but she couldn't
think of a situation in which speaking one
word of English would betray them. She
heartily envied Joe, who sat up front near
the driver and chatted companionably with
him from time to time in Arabic; obviously
they had met before, but she could only look

ahead and number the hours the three of them had to remain silent; she felt deprived and frustrated.

When the bus pulled into the station at Tadmor, Mrs. Pollifax drew her headscarf closer and turned her face away from the window. This was the bus station that she and Farrell had hoped to reach—it felt a century ago—and not far away there would be the alley down which they'd plunged into disaster. She prayed no soldiers or police would enter the bus to check the passengers, but as the bus emptied it was mostly tourists who climbed in, a noisy group of Germans, free to talk and laugh, and Mrs. Pollifax hated them for that freedom.

How surly I'm growing, she thought, *but how lovely to be a carefree tourist.*

However, with Damascus only three hours away now she closed her eyes and tried to picture the shops in the Damascus souk they had passed, and that she had tried to memorize, as they left Omar's carpet stall. . . . Copper pots she could remember, and two large photos of President Assad, one smiling and one serious, each suspended overhead, but there had been other details, and what were they? In the labyrinth

of alleys there had been so many shops selling rugs, which left only the smiling and serious Hafiz al-Assad photos to find.

Needle in a haystack, she thought, and
then . . . *Sheepskins, yes: vests and rugs.*
And with this she had to be content.

Before reaching Damascus she distrib-
uted the dates and grapes that Barney had
presented to her at the last minute, and Farrell brought out the bread that Joe had contributed, and the food had a soothing
effect—it had been a long time since they'd
eaten—and when they reached the *Station
d'autobus* in Damascus they had consumed
every crumb of bread and every grape. Joe
was the first off the bus and lingered nearby,
frequently glancing at his watch as if meeting someone. After Mrs. Pollifax, Amanda,
and Farrell had made their exit he began
strolling out of the square and into the
street, with them following him at a discreet
distance. Several blocks later he turned to
the right, and with relief Mrs. Pollifax, grip-
ping Amanda's arm, recognized Martyrs'
Square; they were on familiar ground now
and close to the Old City.

It was precisely 9:10 by Mrs. Pollifax's
watch when they walked through the en-

trance to this main covered market, the Souk Al Hamadye, and into the same crowds and lively music as before, the same shouts of the merchants and enlivening atmosphere of a Middle East marketplace. Now it was Joe who fell behind them, giving only a faint smile of acknowledgment as he retreated to allow them to lead the way. Amanda was obviously enchanted by this maze of streets; her face glowed as her eyes moved from displays of daggers, frilly children's clothes, fruit stalls and djellabas; this was certainly not Roseville, Pennsylvania, thought Mrs. Pollifax, giving her a smile.

It was half-past the hour when, as they passed still another alleyway, a barbershop caught Mrs. Pollifax's eye and she abruptly stopped. *Of course—the barbershop,* she remembered, the one detail she'd forgotten, and nudging Farrell she glanced behind her to be sure that Joe was close behind them before she led them into the dim and narrow street.

She counted the shops . . . barber, sheepskin rugs, copper pots, with Omar's stall the fourth, and—"Oh no." She gasped aloud, for the fourth shop was closed, shuttered by a locked steel gate.

Amanda looked at her questioningly. Joe, forgoing caution, said, "What's wrong? Are you sure this was the place?"

"This has to be it," whispered Mrs. Pollifax, and then, "Look, there's the same narrow stone-walled passage next to it—and there's that carved wooden door halfway down the alley, see? This *has* to be the place." *If only he is there,* she thought, and said grimly, "We have to try." *And hope,* she added silently.

With as much casualness as they could summon they strolled down the passageway to the door and knocked. There was no response and Mrs. Pollifax knocked again, and then a third time, until it suddenly opened.

It was the boy Abdul who stood there, and his eyes widened in astonishment. *"You?"* he faltered, recognizing Joe, and he glanced quickly up and down the alley before he looked at Joe's three companions. "But—*min?*"

"He asks who you are," translated Joe.

"Americans, all of us," Mrs. Pollifax told Abdul. "You know us, we met at the Citadel on Monday, at noon, and you gave us tea, and—"

A voice behind the boy said, "Let them in—*quickly,* Abdul," and with relief they entered, the door closing behind them.

The man who had called himself Omar sat at his desk, his profile briefly illuminated by a desk lamp until he reached out and switched it off. Rising, he said curtly, "You wish me stabbed in the back, too? How did you find me? Were you followed? And who are these other people?"

Without invitation Mrs. Pollifax sank into one of his chairs, saying, "We have no idea why the man in Palmyra was attacked. He really is dead?"

He nodded grimly.

"As for these two people, this young man—"

Joe broke in to say, "Abdul can vouch for me, sir, he and I meet twice a month—on Wednesdays—at the Al-Arabi restaurant. I'm Joe Fleming from Tell Khamseh."

Omar's eyes narrowed as he coolly observed Joe, and then his glance moved to Amanda. "And she—this girl—is she worth the death of a valued scholar such as Fareeq Wazagani?"

"Death?" gasped Amanda. "Oh, not another death? Who—what's happened? Who *are* you all?"

To Amanda Mrs. Pollifax said, "Later," and to Omar, sternly, "This is Amanda Pym, the young woman we were sent here to find. Two months ago she saved the lives of two hundred and three people," she emphasized, "on the plane that was hijacked to Damascus. She was kidnapped at the airport."

He bowed his head to Amanda. "Then I beg your pardon. The pleasure of forgiving is sweeter than the pleasure of revenge, but I say frankly I would have been happy to kill you until I learned it was not the police who murdered my friend Fareeq. I mourn him. It is apparent you must have some unknown value—to *them,* whoever they are—and I trust it equals the loss of Fareeq."

"But who is Fareeq?" stammered Amanda.

"She knows nothing, nor do we," Mrs. Pollifax told him. "We've not been able to talk to her at all yet. When we first found her she was drugged and confused, and after that, traveling as Bedouins, none of us dared speak to each other in English without giving ourselves away as Americans."

"I see," he said, and spoke rapidly to Abdul in Arabic; the boy nodded and disappeared.

Joe said, "He's told Abdul to see if any suspicious men—or police—are loitering outside, or nearby."

Amanda shook her head. "It wouldn't be the police—not for *me.* They'd *never* tell the police I'm gone."

"Interesting," said their host, looking at her. "Why?"

But Amanda only shook her head.

Abdul reappeared to say, "Is okay."

"Taib! Then bring us tea and another chair, Abdul," and to the others, "One may ask where you found this young woman?"

"In a camp in the desert. A sniper's camp," said Joe.

"Sniper's camp!" He looked startled, and turned to Amanda to ask, "And for what reason were you there?"

She only looked at him, saying nothing.

"Our lives are in his hands," Mrs. Pollifax told her quietly. "He can be trusted; you *must* trust him—we're trying to get you out of the country."

Amanda said reluctantly, "I was being taught to kill."

"And who were you being trained to kill?" he inquired.

She shook her head. "Please," she whispered.

"Please?" His voice was cynical.

"Does it matter?" she asked in a depressed voice. "They said a name but not one I knew. And who would believe anyway?"

"Try us," said Farrell.

Amanda looked around like a trapped animal. "Not here, oh *please* not until I'm safe." Tears filled her eyes. "They threatened me every day, gave me pills to sleep every night, they'll kill me if they find me."

Omar gave her a sharp glance. "A very unlikely story, a young woman and an *American* being trained as an assassin? Of course no one would believe." Turning to her he said rapidly in English, "What weapons did they give you to shoot?"

She said bitterly, "An old VZ 58 V Assault rifle, and sometimes a new SKS rifle."

Surprised, he said, *"Bikeffi—*enough—almost I can believe a little, yes." He eyed her curiously. "But why *you*?"

She lifted her tearstained face and said angrily, "Because—because at first they were going to kill me—they said it was I who shot one of the two hijackers on the plane; he was Ghadan's lover and one of their men. But I didn't kill him, I didn't." She gestured helplessly. "That's when I told them to go ahead anyway and kill me because I didn't care. And I didn't."

"No," said Joe.

"No?" she repeated, startled.

"No."

She gave him a curious glance and said nothing, but continued to give him quick, puzzled glances.

"And then?" asked Mrs. Pollifax.

"That was when Zaki talked to the others and they decided I could be more useful to them alive. To save—to replace—someone named Jizar. 'Expendable' was the word they used for me." Having said this she burst into tears, and Joe walked over to stand beside her chair protectively.

"Zaki," murmured Omar, frowning. "Do you know his last name?"

Sobbing, she shook her head.

Farrell said gently, "At some point you really *must* tell us who they were planning to assassinate."

She lifted her face to say, "Not until I'm

safe, not until I'm out of this country. Please—I will, I will, but not here, not yet. I was so frightened on the bus, afraid they'd be waiting—"

"Wallahi!" exclaimed Omar. "Bus? By God, you came by bus to Damascus? Madness!"

"But the only way," pointed out Mrs. Pollifax.

He gave her an exasperated glance. "I say again it was madness, God forbid it happen again! Allah favored you but there are *ghufara*—watchmen—everywhere. The embassy has asked the police to look for you, the hotel has placed your luggage in storage, and Fareeq has been murdered after speaking to you? You have lived a charmed life to get here at all."

Farrell said dryly, "Not quite so charmed. Soon after speaking with your friend Fareeq in Palmyra I was seized in an alley and spent a number of hours tied up and beaten. The Duchess here—we do not speak of names?" he inquired, nodding to Mrs. Pollifax. "She was badly hurt trying to help me."

"Kif? That is, how?"

"She'll have to tell you—they shoved a bag over my head. But they were not police;

what they wanted me to tell them was why I thought Amanda Pym was alive, how I'd learned this, and where I was going to look for her."

Pointing to Mrs. Pollifax Omar said, "And you? They did not take you, too? But no, they would not," he said, answering his own question with a wry smile. "You would be thought to know nothing, being a woman."

"So insulting," murmured Mrs. Pollifax.

"But how fortunate for you," he reminded her, and with a glance at the bandage still on her head, "But what . . . ?"

"A very kind woman treated my bleeding head, and arranged a ride to Tell Khamseh, with a cousin who was delivering supplies to As Sikhneh, and since Fareeq had already given directions . . . But Amanda is shivering," she pointed out. "Can you help us get her out of the country? She has no passport, no identity, she's frightened, and they must be desperate to find her if she knows too much."

"Whatever she knows," said Farrell dryly.

"One wonders," mused Omar, and then, "Her terror I understand but if she leaves here without telling me anything, and they find her—Allah forbid—we will never know who or what they planned. What is to be done? To lose such information . . . let me think."

Abdul brought in fresh tea and a bowl of hummus and bread and placing these on the desk regarded Omar anxiously.

Omar, frowning, said thoughtfully, "It may be possible to smuggle you across the border into Jordan. But very dangerous, and if caught . . ." He stared at Amanda, considering this. "In exchange, there has to be more; I *must* know something. You do not trust me because I am foreign to you, and a stranger, but I am ready to help all I can. But I must know *something*."

She lifted her face and said drearily, "Ghadan said—she was my guard— Ghadan said it is a camp to train mercenaries for the war in Sudan in Africa. There was a Frenchman named Andre—oh how he loved guns," she said with a shiver. "And an Englishman they called Bert. And Youseff, Ibrahim and Nehhab—they were Arabs, like Ghadan—and the cook, a black man named Arego. And Zaki, of course—he was the man in charge."

"Half of the people in the Sudan are Muslims—in the north," said Omar, frowning. "At the camp did they never speak English? Did you overhear anything about the Sudan or about Muslims?"

She nodded. "I heard the words *ikhwam muslimin;* I remember Zaki using those words a lot to Ibrahim—yes and to Nehhab."

"Ikhwam muslimin!" Omar looked puzzled. *"Ikhwam muslimin* is the name of the Muslim Brotherhood and *that* is startling, yes. It must be a mistake. If President Assad knew—he does not think kindly of the Muslim Brotherhood, he would never have permitted . . . ." His face tightened and he said roughly, "Get her out of here. There's an American in Jordan. She may feel safe enough there to talk, and whatever she says will be returned to me. You'll find him in Amman in the office of the CIA."

"Rawlings?" said Farrell.

"You know of him?"

Farrell smiled at Mrs. Pollifax. "We've met him, yes, on a previous trip to the Middle East."

Omar nodded. "You must remain in Bedouin disguise, and you," he told Joe, "you, too, must be a Bedouin. I can arrange for you to go south with one of several other

Bedu, but *not* by bus! There is a connection in Bosra if I can get you there."

"Bosra!" exclaimed Joe, reaching for the guidebook that Mrs. Pollifax had entrusted to him. "But that's over a hundred miles from here!"

"Oh yes," agreed Omar, "but Bosra is only forty kilometers from the Jordan border."

"I see," breathed Mrs. Pollifax, understanding the shape of his thoughts. "The border."

"You cannot of course cross at Der'a, the official crossing point, but it may be possible some miles to the north—Alghariyeh, for instance. The contact at Bosra will know—he is a smuggler, he does it *only* for money, he is not political, he knows nothing of me—but I have a source who can send word to expect you."

"Is he reliable?" asked Mrs. Pollifax doubtfully.

"Only if you have enough money," he said.

Farrell nodded. "We have money."

They waited patiently, and in much suspense, because none of this sounded possible but they were entirely in Omar's hands.

Looking them over, one by one, he sighed. "I see three of you with good USA passports. A pity one of you could not officially cross the border at Der'a and reach Mr. Rawlings, who might help."

They looked at each other, startled.

"But no," he said wearily. "They already look for you"—he nodded to Farrell and Mrs. Pollifax—"and for this young man you came with, this one with the eyeglasses. He is the only one of you who speaks Arabic. *Hâda mâ bísir!*"

"He means impossible," contributed Joe.

Mrs. Pollifax breathed a sigh of relief.

Omar glanced at his watch, an ornate gold affair. Obviously he prospered as a merchant, and she thought of how much he risked by the secret work he did, and of the men and women all over the world who lived similar lives, some out of patriotism or for an ideal, some for money, others for revenge, or, like Farrell, who simply enjoyed the challenge of living dangerously.

But then there was Fareeq, except she didn't want to think of him just now, not when there was no knowing if they would meet a similar fate.

Omar appeared to reach a decision. "I

would like to see you out of this country by night," he said, and with another glance at his watch, "It is three minutes to ten o'clock. You have traveled all night, you will rest here while I find arrangements. With luck you can be at As Sweida by one or two o'clock, but from As Sweida to Bosra you will be on your own, there are no connectings. While I am gone you must be very quiet and speak only in low voices. As for me," he added, "I must see how quickly I can get you out of here. Abdul, before you open the shop, they will need shabbier robes, such as the *abaya* the girl and your Duchess wear. You said you have money?"

Both Farrell and Mrs. Pollifax nodded, and Mrs. Pollifax reached into the pocket that she'd sewn into her *abaya* and brought out a handful of bills.

"*Taib*—give Abdul a few. Before I leave, Abdul, go to Naima's stall; I saw yesterday she has a few *burqas* to sell. Buy one. For you," he explained to Mrs. Pollifax. "This is the black veil that covers all but the eyes. Not comfortable but concealing. At each call to prayer you must place your white scarf on the head and kneel to pray, like a true Muslim. And from our trunk, Abdul, bring out two of our oldest *abayas*. But you," he said, pointing to Joe, "those eyeglasses, they will have to go. Abdul?"

Abdul nodded and went out, returning soon with an armful of black cloth, after which Omar spoke to him in a low voice and left, not by the door, but through the curtain that apparently masked an inner room they were not to see.

14

When Omar had gone Amanda said timidly, "This Fareeq who's been killed, it had something to do with me?"

Farrell nodded. "We think he was killed by someone from your sniper camp who had been following us."

"Following you?" she said, bewildered. "But why?"

Mrs. Pollifax said, "The embassy in Damascus has given you up for dead, but certain rumors reached intelligence in the United States that you were still alive, or might be, which is why Farrell and I were sent here to find you. We were told we'd have help once we got here—and Omar was our first contact. Incidentally," she added, "I'm here as an aunt of yours, or so the embassy believes."

Joe said, "But Fareeq? You haven't explained *him*."

"No, not even to you," said Farrell, and to Amanda, "Omar didn't have any idea of where you might be—he had only received and reported the rumors—but he said if we went to Palmyra he could arrange for a man to speak to us while we were touring the ruins, a man who would know—oh hell, this gets complicated—but off we went to Palmyra and a stranger *did* pause a few minutes to quietly give us directions to an archaeological camp in the desert. Unfortunately, about ten minutes after he'd spoken with us there were screams from the tourists there and we saw that our informant had been stabbed. That's when we feared it was because he'd been seen stopping to talk to us, and that's when we guessed we were being followed, but *not* by the police."

"There's no need to go into the rest," said Mrs. Pollifax dryly. "We *were* being followed—by two men in djellabas who caught up with us later. And they knew, somehow, precisely what we were up to, and they did *not* want us to find you."

Amanda said in surprise, "Two men in robes? What day?" and when they told her she said slowly, "Nehhab and Youseff left camp early that morning—they looked so funny in those robes when mornings they wore shorts and T-shirts. They still hadn't come back, and I wondered what had happened to them."

"Still on the loose, then," said Farrell grimly.

"Good God," Joe said. "So that's why you turned up at the camp in the middle of the night with a bandaged head, and Farrell two days later looking like death itself. They'd already murdered a man? They were really *serious* about killing you?"

Hearing this Amanda said with a gasp, "But that's horrible, I'm not that important—I'm not, I'm *not.* You should have left me back there, you should never *never* have—"

Joe interrupted her to say fiercely, "Oh come off it, Amanda, stop being ready to sacrifice yourself at the drop of a hat. Of course you're important. Why else are we here? No omelet's ever made without breaking an egg or two."

"Omelet?" she faltered.

"Omelet, yes."

She looked at him in astonishment. "Of course—yes, I'm sorry."

"You're tired—stay quiet," he told her, and Mrs. Pollifax found herself smiling. *Perfect,* she thought. Apparently Joe, having studied the scraps from Amanda's journal of her life in Roseville had taken her measure: Amanda was going to be denied guilt and self-effacement. Joe, she thought, was more clever than she'd realized, and possibly Amanda was realizing this, too, because again she gave him a curious and thoughtful glance.

Abdul brought them platters of *khobz* and hummus, saying, "Now I sell for my father in the shop." He added words to Joe in Arabic, who nodded. "He says eat and quickly change into the clothes he brought us, because when Omar returns we have to be ready."

Once he had left, the four of them sat down to eat on the rug he'd spread for them. Mrs. Pollifax, looking across at Amanda, said, "You're not the same person we saw on film being interviewed in the Damascus airport almost two months ago."

Farrell nodded. "Can't be. Humanly impossible."

"True," agreed Joe. "So who are you now, Amanda?"

She looked at them for a long time before she said shyly, "I don't know," and shivered. "There was a film?"

"You were big news—briefly," explained Mrs. Pollifax. "Farrell and I were shown the film again just before we left to come here. You looked . . . older."

"Not very happy," added Farrell. "Miserable, in fact. How do you feel now?"

"Scared," she admitted with an apologetic half smile. "I thought last night I was being kidnapped again. I still don't know who you are, not really."

Joe said boldly, with a grin, "I don't mind introducing myself first. I'm Joe Fleming, junior archaeologist, and just along for the ride, so to speak, because I know Arabic. *They're* the professionals," he said, nodding at Farrell and Mrs. Pollifax.

"But . . . professional what?"

"Finders of Lost Persons Department," Farrell told her flippantly, "and we have every hope of getting safely out of Syria," he lied.

"But we're all scared—a little," Joe told her kindly. "It's more companionable to know that, I think."

Farrell changed the subject quickly.

"Have we eaten enough? I can't wait to see the Duchess in that *burqa.*"

"Duchess?" faltered Amanda. "A real duchess?"

"I call her that," explained Farrell gravely. "We have a long acquaintance."

Abandoning the food to change clothes Farrell and Joe donned the older and shabbier brown *abayas* while Mrs. Pollifax was shrouded in black from head to foot, with only her eyes to be seen. Unfortunately, in abandoning her previous robe, she left Amanda wearing the only one with inner pockets. Alarmed by this, Mrs. Pollifax removed her black *abaya,* shrugged into her brown one with pockets, and then—hoping for cool weather—pulled the black one over it. "Because I'm the bank, I carry the money," she explained to Amanda.

"Do I have pockets?" asked Amanda.

"Yes, she sewed them inside yours, too, bless her," said Farrell.

"She can keep the travel guide and map for us," added Joe, and handed them over to her, and as he said this the rug concealing the mysterious inner room was pulled aside and Omar hurried in.

"Ready?" he said breathlessly.

"Yes, but what has been arranged?" asked Farrell. "You look—"

"Tired," Omar told him. "In two days I was to ship an order of kilims to As Sweida. My driver is just back from a delivery to Aleppo and he is tired, very tired. With a little baksheesh he has been persuaded to drive there today. *Now* . . . to As Sweida, which in miles is twenty-eight from Bosra." He looked them over sternly. "You may have to walk those miles to Bosra; I do not know."

"Does he know who we are?" asked Farrell.

"No. Therefore you cannot bribe him to go farther, if you even see him. You are a poor family without money, friends of friends, who must see a dying relative in the south, I did not say where, and one of you is ill." To Amanda and Mrs. Pollifax he said, "And do not forget to pray, as women here do." To Joe he said, "You already know the call to prayer?"

Joe nodded. "All five: the Maghrib, 'Asha, Subh, Duhr and Asr . . . *Allahu akbar* three times, *ashadu an la ilaha illa-llullah, ashhadu anna Muhammedanar-rasulullah* twice, *hayya 'alas-sala* twice. Facing east, to Mecca."

Omar nodded. *"Taib.* I hear a small accent, thus do not speak it loud. In Bosra you must wait near the Citadel, understood?"

Inspecting them all he nodded. "Come," he said, and lifting the carpet to the room behind them he led them into it. There were huge piles of rugs everywhere, shelves lightly covered with gauze curtains, cupboards, a computer, a telephone. Amanda, walking beside Mrs. Pollifax, looked around her with awe, and when she stopped it was to stroke a soft and velvety roll of plush, and then, curious, she brushed aside a few inches of a curtain over one of the shelves and peeked inside. "Amanda, we must *hurry,"* Mrs. Pollifax reminded her. She walked on, but when she glanced back she thought she saw Amanda slip something into the pocket of her *abaya* but there was no time to chide her for taking something that pleased her from the shelf, because Omar was pulling aside one of the rugs on the floor, a shabby but exquisite Persian, to reveal a trapdoor and below it a ladder that disappeared into darkness.

He said grimly, "The souk is thousands of years old and many have had to flee thus for their lives but you must never never mention this. I learned of it only from studying ancient documents and maps." With a flashlight he directed them down the ladder and then pulled the trapdoor over their heads and took the lead.

There were no lights in the tunnel except for Omar's flashlight dancing ahead of them; they stumbled over uneven ground, the walls of ancient stone damp and lined with lichen. The passage turned only once, quite sharply, and after a few more minutes they reached another ladder leaning against the wall. Omar established it firmly, mounted it, lifted another trapdoor and helped the four of them up and into what appeared to be a storeroom full of oil cans and cartons.

For Mrs. Pollifax it was a relief to see daylight again.

"You are no longer in the souk," he told them. "The truck is outside—come!"

He opened the door to a large truck that had backed so closely to the entrance that it was impossible to see either the driver or the street behind it, only its open rear crowded with upright carpets, tightly rolled and roped together.

A small passage had been left for them to crawl inside. "There is space in the middle," Omar told them. "When you are inside I will restore and secure rugs to hide you," and to Mrs. Pollifax he added, "Allah grant it be well for you."

One by one they crawled in among the carpets to the space left for them in the center, and seeing Omar close up their means of entry and exit Mrs. Pollifax hoped none of them suffered from claustrophobia. On the other hand, it was a humanely shaped area so that Amanda and Joe, seated facing each other, left enough room for both Mrs. Pollifax and Farrell to stretch their legs without touching the younger pair. With a sigh of relief Mrs. Pollifax slipped the *burqa* from her face and said, "I can breathe again!"

"Yes, it's good to see you," Farrell told her with a grin.

The driver shifted gears and they took off for As Sweida with each bump jarring the spine. "No shock absorbers," Farrell said with a sigh.

"At least we're on our way," Mrs. Pollifax pointed out. "Somewhere. At last. And the driver can't possibly hear us talk with all these rugs around us, nothing insulates like a rug. Are you tired?"

"Of course not," snapped Farrell, and promptly fell asleep.

This left Mrs. Pollifax with only her unruly thoughts and worries until she heard Joe say to Amanda very politely, "Was this your first trip abroad?"

Amanda looked alarmed at being spoken to but replied with equal politeness, "Yes." And then, as if considering what travel abroad *usually* meant, she suddenly smiled.

Nothing had prepared Mrs. Pollifax for a smile: she had seen Amanda grim, serious, angry, and frightened but her smile had the radiance of a sun's rising. "But I didn't get very far, did I."

Joe laughed. "No."

Regarding him curiously she said, "How did you seem to guess I didn't care—about living, I mean."

"Bring out the travel guide I gave you to carry in your pocket," he told her. "I'll show you how."

From one of her inside pockets she brought out the small book and handed it to him, and he extracted two loose folded sheets of paper. "Because of this," he said. "You kept a journal. Your kidnappers made a fire at some distance from the camp to burn your passport and everything else belonging to you. They assumed that everything would burn up, but there was a tiny piece of your passport left—Mrs. Pollifax found that—and these charred scraps. I put them together and they . . . well, they made a picture of what your life had been. Or so I assumed."

"Oh," she said, startled, and then, "Oh dear, oh *no.*"

He handed her the two sheets of paper. "I'm sorry. I know journals are very private and it was intrusive of me to read your thoughts but we *had* to find out if you were inside that fenced compound. Which we didn't know until we found that corner of your passport."

Looking at the put-together sentences she said, "But from such scraps and snippets . . . it's embarrassing."

He nodded. "You're blushing and I'm sorry. Usually my work is studying the Umayyads, who occupied Syria from A.D. 661 to 750. It was sort of like archaeology; I was interested in someone my own age leaving behind a script—I mean words. Except," he added humorously, "you weren't an Umayyad. And once I heard about the hijacking I was also curious as to why you just walked up to the nearest hijacker and asked for his gun. I wanted to know what you were like, and who you were."

There was a touch of anger in her voice when she said, "So now you know."

"Exactly," and he added bluntly, "I deduced that your parents were a pair of bloody misers, and didn't allow you to do anything you wanted, in fact they were abusive."

She looked horrified. "Abusive? Oh no, they *never* hit or beat me, never."

He said gently, "There's such a thing as *emotional* abuse, Amanda."

"Emotional abuse?" she said wonderingly.

"Yes . . . indifference, neglect, lack of warmth and loving."

He had shocked Amanda, and she glanced quickly away from him, but although she didn't speak she looked thoughtful, and Joe—*wise Joe,* thought Mrs. Pollifax—said no more, closed his eyes and pretended to sleep. But Mrs. Pollifax noticed that Amanda's eyes kept straying, puzzled, to the sheet of paper in her lap with its strung-together half sentences that de-

scribed a life she'd lived in Roseville, Pennsylvania. But it was worth remembering,
thought Mrs. Pollifax, that she'd planned a
trip to Egypt, and it had taken courage even
to apply for a passport and board a plane.

A few minutes later Joe opened his eyes,
and aware of the travel guidebook still on
his lap said, "Well, let's see what it says
about As Sweida before it goes back into
Amanda's pocket." He opened it, consulted
the index, turned a page and immediately
winced. "The word 'charmless' is the first
word I see."

Farrell said dryly, "Well, we're scarcely
tourists visiting it as sightseers."

"Its history? During Byzantine rule, Arabs
poured over the area," he read, "destroying
and killing, and in the next century streams
of molten lava from hill craters flowed over
it, turning it into a country of black basalt
stones. It is sometimes called 'Black *soi-
udâ*' . . . Sounds gloomy," he added. "And
just as Omar said, no transportation between it and Bosra."

He returned the guidebook to Amanda,
who stuffed it back in her pocket.

"So we walk?" asked Mrs. Pollifax, winc-
ing.

Joe frowned. "You? Absolutely not—there is such a thing as gallantry. Let me nose around the place first. Give me some of your hoard of bills and let me see what I can find."

Farrell said warningly, "Joe, you've got to be *careful*. My God, if you're careless—they're looking for us."

Joe nodded. "But not for me, I don't *think* I'll head for the oldest, poorest section of town. It's unfortunate, but the less affluent people in any town are the very last to hear about people the police want. Trust me."

"No choice," growled Farrell.

"What we must do is find you a wall to sit on not far from this highway and where I can find you. Sit and eat some leftover dates and don't look at anyone."

Amanda suddenly giggled, and they looked at her in surprise. She said apologetically, "I'm sorry; it must be nerves. I mean it's . . . it's . . ."

Mrs. Pollifax patted her hand. "It's not Roseville."

There was no more conversation. The truck bumped and rattled, the sun poured down on them, and there seemed an inordinate amount of dust raised by the truck.

It felt a long journey, although Omar had said it was eighty kilometers. They stopped once, for the noon call to prayer, and an hour later the truck stopped again. This time the driver walked around to the rear, cut ropes and moved rugs to let them out, and without interest spoke only two words in Arabic. Hastily Mrs. Pollifax slipped the *burqa* over her head again.

"He means get out," whispered Joe, "and not too politely, either."

"Shukren," he murmured as they dismounted to find themselves at the edge of the town, but what startled Mrs. Pollifax was to see that the earth lining the highway was bloodred and the stones really were as black as lava. The truck at once drove off in a cloud of dust to some remote part of As Sweida, and they quickly crossed the highway to enter the town. After a short walk they found a low wall of black stones near a gas station, from which hung a picture of Haffiz al-Assad, and a sign stating that the garage sold diesel gas, kerosene and NGK spark plugs.

Here they established themselves, just inside the wall, while Joe left them to scout for some means of transportation. An ancient Suzuki car passed, an old De Soto, three motorbikes, an old Austin car, a truck with a missing hood. A teenage boy with curly brown hair, brown skin, a pair of blue jeans, and sandals peddled past them. "Nice," murmured Mrs. Pollifax, and ate another date.

It grew boring. "We've been here almost an hour, damn it," said Farrell with a glance at his watch. "It's nearly two o'clock."

Amanda said anxiously, "Would he have been arrested?"

Neither of them answered that.

It was ten minutes later when they noticed a native riding a donkey at some distance toward them, and it was another few minutes before Mrs. Pollifax said, "Farrell, can that possibly be . . . ?"

It was. Joe had purchased a mangy, swaybacked donkey for them. "Cost a small fortune, too," he said. "Only one I could buy. But I learned there's a secondary road not far down the highway on the right—through two small villages—that leads to Bosra. It'll get us off the highway."

Farrell said, "Okay, climb on, Duchess."

Mrs. Pollifax regarded the donkey doubtfully: a previous experience riding one in Albania had not proved a happy adventure, but before it was necessary for her to approach the animal Joe said sharply, "No! Farrell rides until we're off the highway. In this country women walk. Later we take turns."

In this manner they left As Sweida, the apparent father of this apparent family riding the donkey, Joe leading it, while Mrs. Pollifax and Amanda trailed behind in the dust.

"But will we get to Bosra before sunset?" asked Amanda anxiously.

Mrs. Pollifax could only hope so, for it was already nearly three o'clock, and they had added a very stubborn and temperamental donkey to their ménage. It was true that a donkey added a decorative touch to their disguises as Bedu, but she could not help feeling that it would have been faster if they had walked to Bosra without him.

"Will we be there in time?" she replied. *"Inshallah."*

15

Once they left the highway for the secondary road their walk was across a treeless plain, the fields on either side of the road cut to stubble from the summer's harvest. "Watermelons, probably," said Joe. "Long since harvested."

They passed an abandoned truck on the roadside, reduced now to a skeleton, and they gave it a wistful glance—oh, to have a truck!—for the donkey was definitely proving to be a frustration, and even Joe had begun to rue the brilliance of his purchase. "He doesn't like us," he said, giving the donkey a reproachful glance. "He balks. He's stubborn."

Farrell said grimly, "He doesn't realize we have a life-and-death appointment in Bosra at six o'clock."

"But he *has* given us a chance to sit," pointed out Mrs. Pollifax, who guessed that blisters were already forming on her feet. "Do you think we *can* make it to Bosra by six?"

"Prod him harder," Farrell told Joe. "What time is it?"

Wearing two *abayas,* one over the over, had proven very hot, but Mrs. Pollifax had been happy to sacrifice comfort for the sake of the pockets in the one, and she brought out her wristwatch. "Oh dear, it's after three o'clock already."

"Leaving us a scarce three more hours, and I'd guess we've covered nine miles—at most ten miles—which leaves eighteen more." He shook his head. "If we could only hitchhike! Sorry, Joe, we've simply got to abandon the donkey; he's slowing us down. We need to walk, and walk fast. And pray."

"We can do both," said Amanda abruptly, "but I notice Mrs. Pollifax's sandals are too small and mine are so big they flap. I think we could walk faster if we trade them."

It was her first contribution, and they welcomed it with surprise. The two pairs of sandals were exchanged, the donkey tied to a rock in hope that someone would soon res-

cue him—"They cost farmers real money,"
said Joe, "he should make someone
happy"—and once Mrs. Pollifax had torn off
shreds of her *abaya* to pad the blisters on
her feet she found that she could indeed
walk faster. But obviously they were not going to reach Bosra by six o'clock, and she
had no idea of what they could do since
they didn't even know the name of the man
who was to guide them to the border. They
must all realize this, she thought, but it was
no time to consider it. At least they could
talk to each other in English, and she inquired of Amanda, "Are you still frightened?"

Amanda hesitated and then, "Not with
you," she said shyly, and suddenly she began to talk, tonelessly at first, as if she was
unaccustomed to forming her thoughts into
words and speaking them. "I was never allowed to be alone," she blurted out.
"Ghadan was always with me, and Ghadan
hated me, really hated me, because she still
thought I'd killed her lover on the plane, except I didn't. . . . And over and over we were
drilled . . . pistols, small guns, and rifles,
and we had to learn how to hide and
camouflage ourselves, and practice noticing

everything—people who might be camou-
flaged, too, or in hiding and waiting—and
Zaki kept score every day of how many
things we'd seen that had been hidden from
us." She added sadly, "I could have tried to
escape—the fences weren't electric—but I
didn't know anything at all about deserts, or
where I was, or where to go . . . and sometimes there were pills; they made me take
them, to quiet me. Make me sleep. I didn't
like that. . . ." And then, as if suddenly moving from Then to Now, she looked startled.
"If you hadn't come for me . . ." she said,
and shivered.

Joe said gently, "But Mrs. Pollifax and
Farrell did come for you, and later me, too.
Are you still scared?"

She said in a small, astonished voice,
"There are still miracles, aren't there?" and
with a smile, "I guess what I feel now is more
like suspense. And just a little *hope.* But for
what I don't know."

"If we get through this," Joe said sternly,
"I hope you're not going to try something
crazy again to get yourself killed."

"It seems so long ago," she said, frowning. "No," she added at last, "I begin to
feel . . . begin to feel . . ." She drew a long

breath. "Not dead inside any longer, or well, trapped."

"You mean like the sniper's camp," Farrell said.

Amanda shook her head, not ready yet, thought Mrs. Pollifax, to speak of a life in Roseville that had led her to—one had to call a spade a spade—an attempt to end her life. Impulsively Mrs. Pollifax reached over and gave her a hug and was startled by her reaction: Amanda was not accustomed to affectionate hugs.

"How about reading to us, Joe?" she said, continuing her attempt to keep them occupied. "Amanda, hand over the guidebook in your pocket and—"

"Yes," said Farrell. "So we can find out where the hell the Citadel is in Bosra. It'll make us walk faster."

She obligingly reached into her pocket and handed the book to Farrell, who glanced at the index, turned pages and skimmed through the report on the town. "It's a 'backwash' now," he read, "but once a very busy place when there were caravans. Still a number of ruins . . . ah, a tiny map, good! The main streets are laid out north to south and east to west in straight lines, and— Hey, it has the best-preserved Roman theater in existence—and this is weird, the Citadel was built around the theater."

"Yes, but where's the Citadel?"

"If we enter by the north gate—if it's still standing—we can walk in a straight line down the main street past a mosque and through a marketplace to the Citadel at the end of the street."

"I like straight lines," said Joe, glancing over his shoulder. "Deliver us from alleys and mazes."

"What's more—" began Joe.

"Car coming," warned Mrs. Pollifax, and Joe quickly returned the book to Amanda to conceal in her *abaya*.

A shabby gray Austin rattled past them with a man driving it who glanced briefly at them and then, not far up the road, stopped his car. Leaving it, he knelt beside it, plunged his hands into the earth to clean them, and then, prostrating himself, appeared to begin his prayers to Allah.

Observing this, Joe frowned. Glancing at the position of the sun in the sky he said, "Something's wrong, it's not time for the

'Asr, it's far too early, and look, he's not even facing east."

"You think he's waiting for us?"

Stoically Mrs. Pollifax said, "We keep walking, there's nothing else to do."

Joe nodded. "Okay, stay casual. Amanda, stop looking so scared."

"Things just keep *happening*," she told him. "Of course I'm scared."

As casually as possible they walked toward the parked car, taking care not to look at the man, except for Joe, who gave him a nod as he rose to his feet.

The man said in English, "I look for four Bedouin on their way to Bosra."

We've been trapped, thought Mrs. Pollifax.

"On way to *Citadel*," he emphasized.

They looked at each other in consternation. They had not expected this.

Joe said, *"Meen hadetak?* Who are you?" and politely, *"Shu btusgtughal Hadertak?"*

"Delil. La tekhaf—do not fear. *Habid*—friend." And losing his patience he said angrily, "For the love of Allah, get into my car. My name is Antun, I have looked and looked for you. There is trouble—come!"

Thoroughly alarmed, as well as confused,

they tugged at the door to the Austin and climbed in.

"*What* trouble?" demanded Farrell.

"I am betrayed," he said. "I must go to Jordan with you *alyum.* Today."

"Betrayed?" echoed Mrs. Pollifax.

With the car in motion he had to shout over its noisy rattlings. "It was three days ago Fuad ibn Zazi came to village, he—"

"Who?" interrupted Joe.

"*Ash-shurta*—police of here. He questions me, do I smuggle people to border? I say I am innocent, but he does not go away, he watches—for three days he has watched. It is now my knowledge that two peoples I take to border one week ago betrayed me, may Allah curse them. So Fuad watches. He waits."

Astonished, Mrs. Pollifax said, "And in spite of that you're still *here*—to take us to the border?"

He said simply, "I need the money you will pay me."

There was logic in this, and Mrs. Pollifax nodded.

"But there is more," he said, frowning. "This morning—early this morning—very *gharib*—"

"Very strange," interpreted Joe.

"Excuse, yes . . . strange. Two men come to the village—strange ones—looking for one man and two women in Bedu clothes, if they have been seen, they ask."

"But we are four," Amanda said quickly.

"And we have not been followed," pointed out Mrs. Pollifax. "I know this, we have *not* been followed."

Antun glanced in his rearview mirror and seeing no traffic he pulled the car to the side of the road and stopped. Turning to look at them he said, "You must tell me where have you come from, you are so sure you have not been followed."

Joe spoke to him at length in Arabic but the only words they understood were *Camp Al-Khamseh, Amanda, As Sikhneh, bus,* and *Damascus.*

Antun frowned. "So you waited on Deir Ez Zor highway for bus at As Sikhneh, at night, up north in desert. Four of you as Bedu?"

There was a startled silence and then Mrs. Pollifax, pointing to Joe, said, "No, he traveled in American clothes."

"So in As Sikhneh there were three of

you," said Antun. "And these *gharib* men look for three."

"But how could they know?" protested Mrs. Pollifax. "We were careful, very watchful, and it was night. I can't believe this."

Antun shook his head. "It is like the hunt for small animals. If you learn the hole they go into you can guess where they will come out. There is no need to follow if enough is known. If you must get to a border to leave Syria there are only four borders: Turkey, Iraq, Lebanon, Jordan, and if you are American it would be Jordan. You waited long at As Sikhneh?"

"Several hours," said Joe.

"For the *Damascus* bus?"

"Yes," said Farrell, looking puzzled.

Antun nodded sadly. "They need only know that. It is this girl they are after?" He gave Amanda a curious glance. "If you were seen there—a woman, a man and this girl—"

"But we weren't seen," protested Farrell.

Mrs. Pollifax said, "No, and I don't understand why you suspect— Oh dear God," she said abruptly.

"Oh dear God *what?*" asked Farrell.

"You were asleep," she told him. "Amanda, too. There *was* a man, the only one who looked, *really* looked at each of us as he passed us. But he didn't get on the bus when it came."

"You didn't tell us," said Farrell.

She said helplessly, "How was I to know? We were at As Sikhneh, miles from Damascus, and a fair distance from where we found Amanda, and disguised, or so we thought. And it was night, and although I watched him he didn't get on the bus with us."

Antun sighed. "We have a saying: 'Man is a target for the accidents of time.' Damascus?" He shook his head. "If they look to you to flee the country Damascus would mean Jordan. And not Der'aa, where tourists cross." He shook his head. "They look for you at small towns near border." His sigh deepened. "The village police are human. A few questions of Fuad and he *might* tell them there is man in Bosra he has learned may smuggle peoples across the border. I do not know if Fuad takes baksheesh but this is always possible. The police in this country—the *mukhabarat* especially—they are Alawis, as is President Assad—and that is all that matters. Some are—what is word, weak? No, corrupt? But Fuad is in Bosra, and the two men were here in the village, early."

"What . . . what," faltered Amanda, "did those two men look like?"

"They were all legs. They wore shorts, like tourists." He shook his head in disgust.

Amanda sank back in the car in horror. "From the camp? It sounds as if they must be from the camp. I feel sick."

Antun gave her an alarmed glance. "No, no, they did not stay, they were gone when I left."

"Good," said Mrs. Pollifax, and considering this no time to consider possible complications she changed the subject by saying briskly, "Now what are your plans for us?"

"*No* Citadel. In backseat you note small bag on floor, my best clothes for Jordan and photograph of my dead wife. Keep bag for me. Now *dir bálak.*"

"Pay attention," nodded Joe.

"I leave you at Bal al-Hawa, the western gate, the Gate of the Winds. There is kina tree there for shade. Me, I will restore car to Bosra and at *maghrib—*"

"Sunset," supplied Joe. "After call to prayer."

He nodded. "I go for small walk—and meet you."

"And how far is the border?" asked Farrell.

He shrugged. "A rough walk. Two wadis to cross. Ten miles."

Mrs. Pollifax winced, but Amanda broke in to ask, "Is there a fence at the border? Is it electrified?"

"Yes and yes," said Antun, "but we will not cross where I led the peoples who betrayed me. I have dug a new hole under the fence. *Maalesh,* it is covered with earth, across from a big, big *hájar* shaped like a *beid.*"

"Egg," translated Joe. "A big rock shaped like an egg. But the country's so flat, and so rocky, and without a light to guide us?"

"Me you have to guide," said Antun. "I know the stones." He pointed to the mountain in the east. "That is Jebel Druze, the border we cross is in its shadow and that is when we light a *fânûs* to find the stone. Only then. There are cities up on Jebel Druze: Salkhad, Dieben, Alghariyeh, there will be lights on the mountain."

"But—*fânûs?*" asked Mrs. Pollifax.

"Lantern," explained Joe.

Antun nodded. "This too lies at your feet, I leave it with you to keep safe for us."

The ground ahead of them was changing now, rising out of the valley toward Bosra. They could see the shape of a town, the silhouette of a spire, a line of columns such as they had seen in Palmyra, and ahead of them a large stone arch with the detritus of what had once been a wall scattered across the earth.

"The Gate of the Winds," said Antun, and glanced at his watch. "You would still not be here if you walked; Allah be praised I find you fast!"

He stopped the car beside the arch. "Go," he said. "Not quickly—I have given ride to four weary people, no more. Sit. Be quiet. Rest. And pray at sundown."

Once they were out of the car he rattled away in his dusty Austin down a cobbled street, leaving them to take shelter under the shade of the kina tree that he had promised them.

"So," said Farrell, as they seated themselves on the earth among the bricks of the vanished wall. "We have made it to Bosra . . . He strikes me as a reliable man."

"A desperate one," suggested Mrs. Pollifax. "But he didn't ask for money."

"Not even *rabûn*—earnest money," Joe said. "It would be his right to ask for some when he comes at sunset."

"Yes," agreed Mrs. Pollifax, with a worried glance at Amanda, who had withdrawn from them and looked tense and anxious. She said to Joe, "Talk to us. Tell us something about this country we've scarcely seen. At the Tell Khamseh, Amy Madison told me of the lovely places we were missing."

Joe smiled faintly. "Yes, you've pretty much traveled underground all the way." He too was watching Amanda.

"Can people still write books here?"

"Oh, yes, if they are nonpolitical. Love stories are very popular, often about other eras. One of my favorites is the poet Nizar Qabbani, who left Syria years ago, but ironically—he writes so obliquely—President Assad calls him a national hero. I especially remember a few lines from his *Notes on the Book of Defeat,* supposedly addressed to a long-ago sultan: 'Half your people have no tongues, what good their unheard sighs? The other half, within these walls, run like rabbits and ants, silently inside.'

"Which pretty much applies to the people here, full of unheard sighs. But," he added with a reminiscent smile, "so friendly and generous a people."

"You sound really attached to the place," Farrell told him with a smile.

"It's so full of history," he said simply. "Up north near the Turkish border archaeologists have uncovered what they're convinced is the long-lost Urkesh . . . it's all so biblical. I'm continually astonished to come across places I heard about in Sunday school, and yes," he admitted with a grin, "I was taken to Sunday school as a child, not always happily, but it was a darn good background for an archaeologist, I admit it freely."

It was doubtful that Amanda had heard anything he said, her mind was obviously struggling over the meaning of the two mysterious strangers who had arrived in Bosra that morning. Because Joe had just quoted a line of poetry, Mrs. Pollifax found herself remembering a line from the Emily Dickinson poem that Amanda had brought with her—"I looked in windows for the wealth I could not hope to own"—and she was surprised at how fiercely she wanted to see Amanda placed inside of life, not outside looking at it through glass. The girl had moved from subtle cruelties to malevolent cruelties and she deserved better—if, of course, they successfully crossed the border to safety.

There were no more efforts at conversation; they sat in the heat and dust looking out at the fields over which they must soon make their way, fields of red soil littered with black basalt rocks, although in the far distance she could see a grove of stunted trees offering a small amount of cover. If they could reach them.

She sighed, never enjoying suspense. It held one in thrall, plucking at tired nerves, and she was already tired. She would love to have a warm bath now—how many days had it been?—and then sit down to an American dinner. "Of hot dogs," she heard herself say, and was looked at in surprise by Farrell.

"Hot dogs?" he said. "Are you all right, Duchess?"

She laughed. "Just wistful."

Soon the call to prayer could be heard from the town beyond the gate, and, bringing out her white scarf, she placed it over her suffocating *burqa* and joined Farrell,

Joe, and Amanda in prostrating themselves, with only Joe murmuring the words of the *Sala*. When the prayers' reverberations had died away the last rays of the sun had vanished, leaving them in a brief twilight and Jebel Druze starkly black against the darkening sky. There was a peaceful stillness following the *Sala;* they didn't hear Antun's approach but he was suddenly with them, squatting on his haunches and speaking in a low voice.

"We go first slow, looking for maybe *azhar.* . . ."

"Flowers," said Joe. "Or something lost?" he suggested.

"Na'am. Or *battikh asfar?"*

"Sweet melons," nodded Joe. "I gather they harvested a crop somewhere in those fields."

"You see the trees?" said Antun. "We must go to them before the *kamar*—sorry, before the moon rises high; it will be still bright this night. They grow thick to the *tarik* along the border."

"Tarik?"

"Road," murmured Joe. "Apparently there's a road that runs along the border. For the patrols."

"How often the patrols?" asked Farrell sharply.

Antun shrugged. *"Ma'alesh."*

"He means never mind," Joe explained, and Amanda stood up and said in a strangled voice, "I feel like screaming."

Joe smiled at her and grasped her hand. "But you won't."

She looked at him with widened eyes. "No," she sighed, and drew her hand away. "I'll be all right. Can we please, please *go?*"

"Yes, but first some 'earnest money,' " Mrs. Pollifax said firmly; she was ready for this and passed to Antun half of their remaining Syrian pounds. "The rest once we're across the border."

His round face shone. "So much! I will be rich in my new country—*Shukren!* Oh, I take *taib* care of you!"

"You'd better," murmured Farrell.

"Rich *Amerikâni,*" murmured Joe flippantly.

Antun, excited now, said, *"Yallah!* Let's go!"

Actually, thought Mrs. Pollifax, it was like theater for an unseen audience, should there be one. They walked slowly, stopping to lean over and pretend to pluck something from the earth; they stopped, they pointed, they strolled on, their pace slowly quickening as the town receded behind them. There were three fields to cross, each defined by low walls of black stone, and they were large fields, but the trees ahead grew slowly nearer. The moon that had been full two nights ago was on the wane, but as it rose out of the east it was dismayingly bright. They crossed the first dried-up riverbed, or wadi, and a mile later reached the first gnarled and stunted trees that gave them cover.

"Now," said Antun, "we go *fast.*"

But what Antun had failed to mention was that these were thorn trees, tall, overgrown spiny shrubs with thorns as sharp as needles, rendering it impossible to hurry. There were gasps of "Ouch!" from Amanda, and a few well-chosen curse words from Farrell, and although Mrs. Pollifax was well wrapped in her black shroudlike *abaya* and *burqa,* her hands were soon bleeding as she pushed her way in and out of close-knit groves with Antun pleading with them to go faster, faster.

From time to time the thorn trees mercifully thinned but it felt to Mrs. Pollifax as if they'd been plodding through hell for hours, even days, when Antun abruptly stopped. Placing a finger to his lips he bade them to be still and silent and then, frowning, he nodded and they continued. The moon was high in the sky now and Mrs. Pollifax guessed that it must be nearing midnight. Off to their left, looking up, she could see the pinpricks of light on the Jebel Druze, as Antun had described, but it had begun to be an effort to lift her head; she could only put one foot after another, her eyes on the ground.

At last she dared whisper to Antun, "The border—how far now?"

He stopped, and when he turned to look at her a chance ray of moonlight illuminated his face and she saw that his eyes were glazed with terror. "One mile," he said, and then, "Someone is following us. We are being followed."

"How do you know?" she whispered, alarmed.

"Listen," he said.

She listened but heard nothing.

Farrell and Joe, returning to her side to

ask why they'd stopped, looked at her questioningly.

"He says we're being followed."

"Oh God," murmured Farrell. "What does he hear?"

Joe whispered to Antun in Arabic. "He says he has heard the snap of trees being cut—off to our right—and he has seen birds fly away—and he knows how to listen."

Amanda returned to join them, saying, "What—"

"Sssh," whispered Mrs. Pollifax, and in the silence that followed they could hear at some point behind them the snap of a thorn tree branch, and suddenly Mrs. Pollifax realized that she was the eldest member of this group and that, tired as she was, Carstairs had placed her in charge. When Farrell hissed, "We can't stop like this, we've got to make a run for it," she said, *"No."*

"No?" whispered Antun.

"No," she repeated in a low voice, and to Antun, "If they capture you, Antun?"

He shuddered. "I know too much. Prison."

Joe understood. "Yes, and no doubt torture, whereas we are four Americans, we have an embassy to appeal to—with luck," he added grimly.

"Exactly," she said. "I say we split. If we're being followed they'll follow us whether Antun is with us or not, and he mustn't be found with us. If he steals away alone—with his lantern . . . Antun, you could cross the border and light the lantern for us, couldn't you? So we could find you?" And hated herself for adding, "And pay you the rest of the money? We'll carry your bag for you, too." *Just in case,* she thought.

She had underestimated Antun. *"Na'am*—oh *yes,"* he exclaimed, and there were tears in his eyes. "I am . . . am hit hard by such kindness. I would not fail you, I promise. Take my bag," he said, handing it to her. "It has all my new life in it."

"Thank you," she told him, "and now you must tell us exactly what we must do. We reach the border, the fence, the road and . . . ?"

"Go *dughri*—straight on—to meet road at border. Then half a mile to east—"

"To the left," emphasized Joe.

"Yes, toward Jebel Druze. To the big black rock that shines even in moonlight.

With Allah's blessing I will have dug away *wasakh*—no, *earth*—and light lantern."

"Then go," said Mrs. Pollifax. "Now. Quickly."

"Shukren, shukren," he said, and stepped in among the thorn trees and soon vanished to their left, and at once they resumed their own flight toward the border.

"Who would be following us?" asked Amanda in a desperate voice. "That policeman Fuad?"

"Keep your voice low," counseled Mrs. Pollifax and added, "We seem to have done all that bending over and looking for melons for nothing, if we've been watched from the beginning." A pity, she thought; their performance had been tiresome.

They could hurry now, for the thorn trees were behind them and once again the earth was littered with rocks, and the moonlight was of no help because, perversely, it had disappeared behind a cloud. They reached and crossed the second wadi, met with a scattering of trees, and then suddenly came upon a rough dirt road, and—

"The fence," whispered Amanda. "We've reached the border!"

"Turn left," pointed Joe, "and let's pray Antun has already reached the crossing."

"Half a mile," Farrell reminded them. "He said half a mile. Dare we run?"

"No," said Mrs. Pollifax sharply, and purely from instinct. "We don't know—can't know—if Antun is there."

They stopped to listen for any sounds behind them but there were none. "We've outdistanced whoever it was," whispered Farrell. "We must have."

Unless they picked up Antun's trail, worried Mrs. Pollifax, thinking of the trampled branches and beds of broken thorns that a man in a hurry might leave behind him, and then scolded herself for being so negative.

The moon had surfaced again from behind its cloud as they began their walk down the road, and it was good to feel earth under their feet, with no thorny trees to harass them, and no rocks to skirt. They had covered a fair distance when Mrs. Pollifax saw the flicker of light ahead.

"Antun's lantern!" exclaimed Joe triumphantly. "He's there, he's safely across the border. We can hurry now?"

They hurried.

"And there's the big, shiny, egg-shaped rock," cried Amanda, "Oh, thank God!"

They could also see Antun—he had crossed the border, and he was in Jordan. He stood waiting, dimly illumined by the lantern, but the lantern was not beside him; it had been left on the Syrian side of the fence. At sight of them he screamed, *"Wakkif! Nâs! Hadi 'atteh!"*

Joe gasped. "He says stop—there are men—it's bad!"

"But what—" began Farrell.

It was too late. From behind the egg-shaped rock stepped two men, both Arabs and dressed just as Antun had described them that morning, in shorts, T-shirts and boots.

"Zaki!" gasped Amanda. "And Youseff? Oh to have come so far!"

The taller one stepped forward menacingly. "You think we let you go, you bitch? With what you know?"

So this was Zaki . . . a very distinguished Arab, decided Mrs. Pollifax . . . very military in his well-trimmed mustache, but his lips were thinned now, and his eyes blazing, while the man behind him—Youseff?— looked every bit the subordinate, but his eyes were like a cat's, glittering with triumph; he looked a dangerous subordinate.

They faced each other in the flickering light of the lantern, the moonlight streaming silver over them. Beyond, out of reach, lay the fence and Mrs. Pollifax saw that Antun had cleared his narrow passage under it for them, but he had left the lantern too late.

She turned as she heard the sound of a sharp slap and a cry from Amanda; Zaki had walked over to Amanda and had hit her hard on the cheek. She pressed her hand to it, not looking away but staring at him with narrowed eyes.

"You bastard!" said Joe, and for a moment Mrs. Pollifax thought that Joe was going to attack him, but it was Amanda who hurled herself at Zaki with a tigerlike fury that astonished Mrs. Pollifax.

"I'll kill you," she shouted. "You can't stop me now—you can't, you can't!" Her hands had found his eyes and she was clawing at them while Zaki, taken by surprise—unprepared for assault from a docile pupil—stepped away from her. Viciously he reached out, picked her up and threw her to the ground.

"Brute," shouted Farrell, and at this remark Youseff headed toward Farrell but met instead with Mrs. Pollifax, who stepped forward, seized his arm, and as he turned to confront her she delivered a swift, efficient karate slash to his throat. He sank to the ground, gasping for air and retching, both hands clutching his neck, while Joe, rushing toward Amanda and swearing at Zaki, came to an abrupt halt as Zaki brought out a gun.

Smiling maliciously at Joe he stood over a prostrate Amanda and said, "Well?"

Joe eyed him cautiously. "You really are a devil," he said. "Amanda . . ."

Amanda lay shockingly still, but Mrs. Pollifax, staring at her with concern, saw that she was not unconscious after all, but with one hand she was fumbling inside her *abaya* in an effort to find something, and Mrs. Pollifax's mouth literally dropped open to see Amanda pull out from her *abaya* a gun. *Where on earth did she get that?* wondered Mrs. Pollifax in amazement.

Too late Zaki glanced down at his captive, arrested by her movement, but he had overlooked the pupil he had trained for almost two months. Amanda looked up at him, lifted the gun and shot him twice, once in his left arm, once in his right arm. Stunned, he stared down at his helpless hands, his arms dripping blood, and Amanda, stumbling to her feet, said simply, "I stole it from Omar's cupboard."

Farrell said, "For God's sake, let's get out of here!"

"Yes, go—all of you—*out,*" commanded Amanda, her back to Mrs. Pollifax, Farrell and Joe, the flickering lantern illuminating Zaki dripping blood on the Hawran earth and Youseff on the ground unconscious. "Go—I'll come once you're under the fence and over the border." She did not look at them; her eyes remained on Zaki.

"Not me," said Joe flatly, gesturing Farrell and Mrs. Pollifax to hurry and join Antun. "I stand with *her.*"

Mrs. Pollifax tasted her share of earth as she burrowed and crawled through Antun's narrow passage into Jordan. Behind her came Farrell, who, once upright, shouted, "All clear, you two! Hurry!"

The oil in the lantern on the ground between Zaki and Amanda was perilously low. Together Amanda and Joe backed toward the fence, and Mrs. Pollifax marveled: Amanda Pym might have been frightened of life in Roseville, Pennsylvania, she thought, but what had been overlooked when seen on film, was the girl who had managed a household, worked stoically in a grocery store, learned budgets and repairs, tended an invalid mother, and all without emotional nourishment.

It was interesting, thought Mrs. Pollifax, if not miraculous, to realize that this had given Amanda a strength she'd certainly never realized that she possessed until now.

Amanda was blossoming.

"*Allahu Akhbar,* Allah be praised," said Antun as the last two joined them. "You are in *Jordan* now."

"Amanda, I could kiss you," Farrell said, and to Mrs. Pollifax, "Omar said to look for gypsies encamped not far from the border?"

The lantern on the other side of the fence had run out of oil and the moon had disappeared behind Jebel Druze. Darkness enclosed them, but in the distance they could see a dim light—a lantern, perhaps—and the black silhouette of tents against the night sky. They stumbled toward them, Joe and Antun holding up a shaken Amanda between them, until a different shape could be seen next to the tents; it had the silhouette and lines of a jeep.

Seeing it, Farrell said, "Trouble, Duchess?"

They stopped, suddenly wary, until abruptly the headlights of a car flashed on, then off, then on again, like a signal. A man stepped out of the jeep and shouted, "Mrs. Pollifax? Farrell? I heard shots—my God, is it you?"

And Mrs. Pollifax, recognizing that voice, gave a sob of relief and forgot her exhaustion.

"It's all right," she told them. "Somehow—" Her voice broke. *"Somehow* it's Rawlings—Rawlings, bless him, from the CIA office in Amman."

16

There was an older man in the office with Rawlings when they met the next morning, an American with a tired face and kind eyes who introduced himself as Mr. Smith. He ordered coffee brought to them, or perhaps Miss Pym would prefer a cola?

She smiled. "Oh yes, please."

"I want you to begin at the beginning," Smith emphasized to Amanda. "The *very* beginning: in Roseville, Pennsylvania, for instance. Why you decided on a trip to Egypt, and why you—but let us begin with the 'why' of it all. You'd been unhappy?"

Mrs. Pollifax gave him a curious glance and wondered if Carstairs and the department still cherished suspicions about Amanda.

The girl nodded. "I realize now how angry

and hurt I was; it was such a *shock.*" She hesitated. "It's because I grew up thinking we were poor, you see. There were never any trips or new clothes, always hand-me-downs. It's hard to explain . . . like every night after dinner my mother and father met upstairs in his little office and wrote down every penny they'd spent that day; I learned this after he died, when I had to clear his filing cabinet. It was all there on index cards—years of it. He managed a discount store in Roseville and it turned out that he owned it, but they never told me that. I wanted to go to college—I was even offered a tuition scholarship, but they said no, they couldn't afford the dormitory fees or the books or the travel. Later they said I could start community college if I lived at home, so I registered for that but then my father died. Quite suddenly."

Her face tightened. "After that my mother took to her bed—her heart, she said—and I gave up community college and took a job at the grocery store, at the checkout counter for three hours every morning. Only part-time because it was up to me to look after her, cook, clean, shop, budget."

She added in a toneless voice, "And then

when she died and I went with the lawyer to the safe-deposit box they pulled out stock certificate after stock certificate after stock certificate. And the estate came to nearly a million: it was eight hundred thousand dollars."

She looked up at last, her face sad. "My first thought was what a joyless life they'd lived—and all for *that.* At first I wanted to cry for them, and then—"

"And then," said Mr. Smith, "you wanted to cry for yourself?"

Startled, she said, "Yes. Because they'd left only money, and no love, and I didn't know how to be rich. It was when I stopped trying to save baby dolphins that I realized how depressed I was."

"I beg your pardon?" said Smith.

"Dolphins?" echoed Joe.

She nodded. "Those plastic circles that hold together six-packs of sodas and beers. You didn't know? In the ocean the baby dolphins are attracted to them and they strangle in them, so I've always—*always*—cut up the circles with my scissors. Except I stopped caring even about that."

Recovering from this, Smith said, "And

so—not caring—you decided to travel to Egypt."

She shook her head. "It was the lawyer who suggested it. I think he felt sorry for me."

There was a long silence and then she said, "We were on that plane—on the ground, in Damascus—for so long that I finally understood that going to Egypt wasn't going to change me. I had no idea at *all* what I'd do when I got there, and I'd still be Amanda Pym. And I realized—realized how hopeless everything was, but most of all me."

Mrs. Pollifax wanted very much to intervene but this was Mr. Smith's interview, and she waited.

"So you no longer cared," he said.

"It seems a long time ago," she told him, "but no, I no longer cared."

"And now?" he asked gently, with a smile.

"Now I'd like another chance at living," she told him. "I think I'd like to go to college, although," she added wryly, "I don't suppose knowing how to take apart and clean rifles and pistols would sound well on a résumé, would it?"

"Find a college in New York City," Joe

said eagerly. "That's where I'll begin teaching in February."

She gave him one of her quick, startled glances, and Mrs. Pollifax thought how surprised she continued to be when she was given the acknowledgment and attention she'd never experienced.

Smith said gravely, "Yes, but now we come to what is very important to us: what your abductors planned for you. Can you tell us that now?"

"What they planned for me," she said in a steady voice, "was to use me—instead of one of their men—to assassinate a man who sometimes walked around the grounds of the place where he lived—heavily guarded—and once I became expert at shooting and camouflage I would be a sniper. I was expendable, you see. I would be caught and killed, of course, but it would be Zaki's revenge."

"Revenge?" said Smith. "Revenge on what?"

"On something called Hamah, where every member of his family was killed."

Smith started. "Good God," he said, "are you telling us . . . is it possible . . . ?

Amanda, who were you being trained to assassinate?"

"Mr. Hafiz al-Assad, the president of Syria," she said.

There was a stricken silence that lay heavily on them, and then Farrell said, "My God—thrown to the lions!"

But Joe went to Amanda and stood behind her chair.

Smith said incredulously, "Did they really, honestly, believe that *you* could do that?"

"Why not?" she said bitterly. "What difference did it make, they said, male or female, once I was trained for eighteen hours a day, and I'd already told them to go ahead and kill me, I didn't care. They had aerial photographs of the grounds, they'd found an old map, they seemed to know where a sniper could hide. They made it sound easy."

"There had to have been a few bribes," Smith said flatly. "Otherwise . . ." In a gentler voice he explained to her, "The Muslim Brotherhood, the president's most dangerous opposition for years, was rooted in Hamah. Hamah is a city, Miss Pym. The Brotherhood did their own killings—guerilla attacks on soldiers, government people—

until eventually Assad cracked down on them by wiping out half the population of the city. It was a terrible massacre. Many of the surviving Brotherhood fled to Germany."

"Germany?" repeated Farrell with a start. "One of their men used some German words, the ones who captured me."

Mrs. Pollifax said, "And if this crazy plan had succeeded?"

Smith walked over to the window and stood with his back to them. "Let me put it this way," he said. "In the past decade or two there have been civil wars, massacres, insurrections, and violence throughout the Middle East: in Iraq, Iran, Morocco, Syria, North and South Yemen, and in territories occupied by Israel. Iran and Iraq fought a bloody war for ten years. Israel bombed targets in Iraq, Tunisia, and Lebanon, and invaded Lebanon. The Palestinians began throwing stones, and the intafadal was born; Iraq invaded Kuwait, which began the Gulf War, and I scarcely need point out that this involved America for the first time in a Middle East war.

"In whatever peace can be established in the Middle East," he continued, "al-Assad is a lynchpin: he matters. Never mind what one thinks of him, he wants peace—on his own terms, of course—but he does want peace, and at the moment Syria is an island of comparative stability. Replace him and God only knows what furies might be released."

"Which is what Zaki wanted," added Amanda, nodding. "The furies. I'm sorry but I never knew—about the Middle East, I mean."

Smith said dryly, "In the future I fear it will need a great, great deal of attention." He nodded. "It was wise of you to insist on being out of Syria before you spoke of this. Even our American Embassy there might have found this unbelievable and assumed you were delusional. Now there are four of you as witnesses to where you were found, and your testimony to be sworn to. It will be a matter for the State Department to tactfully and officially explain to President Assad what he unknowingly permitted in his desert. *Not* mercenaries training to fight in the Sudan—half of the Sudan is populated by Muslims, and some of your group may very well be there for that purpose—but a bitter, angry member of the Muslim Brotherhood, the *ikhwam muslimin.*"

"That name again," said Amanda, nodding.

"A group," he added, "that at the moment is doing its best to destabilize Egypt. Now . . . you all had a good sleep last night? You are rested?"

They nodded.

"I am going to put you on a plane tonight for New York. Miss Pym has no passport but I have wired for the number of her passport and once in New York—"

Here Mrs. Pollifax interrupted him. She said, "I reached my husband Cyrus last night by phone," she told him. "He's meeting us at Kennedy Airport with hotel reservations for the four of us to spend a few days in New York. To buy Amanda new clothes and show her around Manhattan."

Farrell said sternly to Joe, "And you, young man, will take her to a nightclub."

"Gladly," said Joe, smiling at her.

Amanda looked at him shyly. "Really?"

"You're also invited to come back to Connecticut with Cyrus and me for a few days— if you'd like," continued Mrs. Pollifax. "Kadi Hopkirk often spends weekends with us, and I think you'd enjoy meeting her because she's about your age and lives in New York, where she studies art."

Amanda's face glowed. "All that? So much?"

"As for the clothes-buying expedition," Joe said firmly, "I shall insist on going along to be sure you buy a few sleek, bright and really dashing outfits, as befits any sniper-trained guerilla. I mean, how can you top *that?*"

Smith cleared his throat and looked rather helplessly at Rawlings.

"Yes," said Rawlings, grinning, "I think we have all the information we need for now. As for your guide, Antun, he's in good hands. He smuggled enough people into Jordan to have a fair number of helpful friends. As you seem to have acquired also, Miss Pym."

Amanda smiled at him gratefully.

"So we'll return you now to the Jordan Intercontinental and I'll pick you up personally at six o'clock for the airport."

Even Farrell nodded happily at this, and as they rose to leave the office he said in an aside to Mrs. Pollifax, "Duchess?"

"Yes?"

"Amanda and Joe . . . think they'll end up marrying?"

"I don't know about that," said Mrs. Pollifax thoughtfully, "but after what they've gone through, and what they know about risks and dangers—and each other—I would guarantee they'll be the best of friends for the rest of their lives."

"As we've become, you and I, Duchess," he said gravely, and reaching for her hand he tucked it under his arm as they followed Amanda and Joe out of the building. "But I'm still willing to bet any amount there'll be a wedding for those two before the next year ends."